NOW YOU KNOW HOW IT FEELS

K.M. SCOTT

Now You Know How It Feels is a work of fiction. Names, characters, places, and events are the products of the author's imagination. Any resemblance to events, locations, or persons, living or dead, is coincidental.

2024 Eight Feathers Press

Copyright © 2024 Eight Feathers Press

All rights reserved. Without limiting the rights under copyright reserved above, no part of this publication may be reproduced, stored in or introduced into a retrieval system, or transmitted, in any form, or by any means (electronic, mechanical, photocopying, recording, or otherwise) without the prior written permission of the copyright owner.

No part of this book may be used or reproduced in any manner for the purpose of training artificial intelligence technologies or systems. In accordance with Article 4(3) of the Digital Single Market Directive 2019/790, and expressly reserve this work from the text and data mining exception.

ISBN: 978-1-947705-04-3

Published in the United States

They say a different version of you exists in the mind of everyone you meet. To some, you're the sweetest, friendliest person in the world. To others, you're that quiet soul who rarely makes a peep.

And to a few, you're a villain.

Carey Mitchell has one more version of herself out there. One that makes someone want her dead.

First, though, they want to ruin her life by framing her for the murders of people close to her. To the police, Carey is the only link between the victims. She's an obvious suspect, no matter how much she claims to know nothing about who's to blame.

The moment is coming when Carey will find out who the killer is. Will the police solve the crimes first, or will she come face-to-face with the person who wants her dead?

1

Private Message

You walk around town, cheerfully enjoying your day and thinking all is right with the world. For a moment, you close your eyes while you wait for the stoplight to change, letting the sun warm your skin on this beautiful May day. That's good. Savor how that feels. You deserve to be so content, right?

You stop at that little café you adore just like you do every workday. We humans do love our lives to be regular, don't we? We loathe boring predictability, but what would your late afternoon break be like without that dose of caffeine from that special coffee shop with that extra shot of caramel and dollop of whipped cream you so love?

See, no matter how random or unpredictable you may think you are, you're very much like everyone else. You take the same route to work every day. You take your break at the same time every workday. You visit the same stores every time you go shopping. It's the sameness that gives you comfort.

But what if that comfort is the very reason you're in danger?

When you sneak a peek at how you look in the store window as you pass, don't believe nobody saw you. You're never truly alone.

Because someone is always watching you.

You don't notice me observing every place you go, every person you speak to, every move you make. The person in the business suit who looks like anyone on the sidewalk of any city catches your eye. Perhaps he's a businessman. Or maybe she's a lawyer. Or they could be a stockbroker.

No, they're none of these things. But they look like they could be, so you don't give them a second thought if you see them near you on the sidewalk. Just another nine-to-fiver in a suit with a briefcase climbing the ladder of success and hoping to reach the top of the mountain, just like you.

At least that's what that little voice in your head tells you.

You nod as you pass the sandwich guy on the corner, giving him a big smile as he waves at you. "Italian today?" he calls out, remembering your favorite guilty pleasure you've sworn off as of last week because your stomach has been giving you problems.

"No, thank you," you say as you shake your head, smiling even broader as you reflect back on the last time you had one of his delicious sandwiches. They are so tasty, and he's such a nice old man, so you add, "Next week!" You don't mean it, but you were brought up to believe it never hurts to be nice.

He nods, happy to hear you'll return, but it won't happen.

You see, with every step you take, someone is right behind you. They've had eyes on you for days now. They know where you're going, what to anticipate, and when you'll be alone.

When the moment's right, that's when it will all end for you.

Why, you might ask, if they gave you the chance to speak in those final moments. Why me? Well, that's easy.

You angered the wrong person. Can't imagine who? Think on it for a little bit.

Was it that office frenemy you forgot to include when that woman retired, a slight he or she has never forgiven you for? It was a simple mistake, and you made sure to fix your error almost immediately, so how could anyone truly blame you?

Or was it the person you treated like shit and then abandoned, sure they weren't even worth a decent goodbye? That kind of thing never leaves someone's mind, you know.

Perhaps it's someone you've never even met. A woman your ex-boyfriend left for you who's finally decided she can't let you live knowing he chose you over her that one night you felt weak and lonely. Or it may be the person your boss promised your job to but gave it to you instead.

That's the thing. How can you know what someone's

thinking? How can you know how desperate anyone is at any given time?

You can't. Every day is a crap shoot. One day, you're on top of the world. The next, you're lower than a snake's belly and looking up at everyone else doing so much better than you.

But don't worry. You won't suffer. Unlike you, I'm not cruel and thoughtless.

You walk out of your office building as dusk falls over the city. You worked late today, probably trying to brown-nose your boss in the hope you'll get a better raise this year. You won't, but it won't matter because someone else has a very different goal for you today.

Killing you.

There will be no reprieve. That's not possible. Not after what you've done. The judge and jury have already decided your fate after hearing all you're guilty of and have pronounced the verdict.

Now it's simply a matter of you dying.

I promise you won't suffer. That would be cruel, and cruelty isn't the name of this game. But you know something about that, don't you?

Then the pretending starts. People seem to mourn, some only play-acting but it's a necessary show. They feel bad for a brief moment in time and then move on. That's life.

And death.

Others wonder how this could happen to such a lovely person. They silently rage against the viciousness of this world where such an innocent soul could be murdered while criminals walk the street free. It seems so unfair.

Then again, how innocent were you?

And still others quietly question who would want someone like you dead. Most people never figure out it's someone who's been there all along. Someone who's sat next to you day after day in the coffee shop without you even caring. Someone who made it their business to pay attention to every move you make. Someone who's fantasized about how they're going to take you out of this world.

If you're lucky, there may be a person or two who genuinely miss you when you're gone. They'll think of you and smile at all the memories they have of the fun times. For them, the question isn't why you had to go but why so young.

None of that matters, though. The end has been determined.

That day is your last day in this world. You will have no more chances to make things right. How things are at that moment is how they'll remain for the rest of eternity.

When will it happen? Hard to say. Don't worry, though. There's nothing you can do. Your fate is set.

The parking lot has an eerie silence to it tonight, broken only by the sound of your shoes tapping on the concrete as you leisurely stroll to your car. The person you didn't notice as you made your way from the building makes no noise, but with every step, they watch to see if you'll turn around.

You don't, though. You're too lost in thought about all

those things you want to do when you get home to sense someone's right behind you. That's a mistake.

They know exactly how long they have before you start that car of yours. You see, you're a creature of habit, much like every other person in this world. You do the same things over and over without even being conscious of them, never thinking those very actions may leave you vulnerable.

For example, every night after work when you get into your car, you leave your doors unlocked and don't immediately drive away. Instead you check your makeup and search for a good song to listen to on the way home.

That's a mistake. In those moments is when you're at your most helpless in this dimly lit parking lot.

That older car a few spots away gives you the impression that you're safe. You aren't alone. There's someone else, someone like you who's done with work for the day and ready to start the ride home, just as soon as they get settled in.

But you're wrong. There's no safety. No protection from someone who's hell bent on killing you.

You take your focus off the rearview mirror, finished with reapplying your lipstick or checking to make sure the lettuce from the chicken wrap you had at lunch isn't still in your teeth, and that's when they strike. You didn't lock the doors, of course. Why should you? This parking lot may be a little frightening, but nothing bad has ever happened here.

Believing that is yet another mistake.

When the person who's watched you for so long finally makes their move, you're so stunned you don't even scream. The only noise is the chiming sound your car makes to alert you that your door is open. For a moment, fear fills your eyes, but then, the last thing they see in them is confusion. The human mind just can't grasp the idea that anyone would do this to another person.

After only a few seconds, it's over. It only takes that long, and that's it. You slump over the wheel, and that person you didn't notice watching you calmly closes the car door, silencing the chiming sound.

That's how life is. One minute, you're alive and looking forward to a relaxing night on the couch with Netflix, and the next you're dead. But did you ever truly live? Wasn't your life just a boring series of routine events that happened again and again?

Every day you went to the same job, drank the same coffee from the same shop every day at the same time, walked the same sidewalks to the same places. You spoke to the same people, saying the same words, and thinking the same thoughts day after day. You loved how settled your life had become, as if you'd achieved something by never trying anything new.

While all along, someone wanted to take that same life from you.

And you never saw it coming.

Something to mull over, don't you think, Carey?

Until next time...

2

My boss may take the prize for the worst boss in the world. The man has no concept of personal space or personal time. He's the director of a toy museum, but the man doesn't possess an ounce of joy one would associate with anything involving children. Worse, he seems hellbent on making my life difficult with his constant popping into my office to demand I do tasks that are technically part of his position.

But the worst part of having Randall James as a boss is I no longer have a life outside of work. The man is practically a stalker after I leave the museum for what's supposed to be my time off. Nights, weekends, even before work in the morning when I'm trying to wake up with a cup of coffee. He doesn't care. If a thought creeps into his mind about something at the museum he thinks we need to discuss, he's right there lighting up my phone.

I stare at the clock on my laptop waiting for the time to change to five o'clock, even though I know the moment I leave my desk, Mr. James will be texting me about something involving work. My friends tell me I should just ignore him, but I need this job and don't know what he'll do if I suddenly become unavailable after work hours.

4:59.

Just one more minute and then it will be the weekend. Yes, I know that doesn't really mean much since my boss will likely be calling me within an hour, but I like to fantasize that this will be the weekend he leaves me alone.

My phone vibrates across the top of my desk, and I see it's Emory. She probably wants to know if we're going to see Jenna tonight. Our mutual friend who works the opposite hours we do as a chef at the hottest restaurant in town, she's rarely around since she took that job, so we have to go to her if we ever want to see her. For everyone else in town without a reservation, the chance of getting into Remington's is a surefire no, but since we know someone behind the scenes, it's at least a possibility. We haven't seen Jenna for nearly two weeks, so maybe we should pop in and see how she's doing.

5:00. I'm free! Well, technically, if not truly free.

I close my laptop and stand from my desk to grab my sweater in preparation for heading out the door for my two days off, but like clockwork, Mr. James appears in my office doorway to talk to me about something that absolutely, positively can't wait until Monday. This guy kills me.

One of these days I'm going to ask him if he honestly believes any of his questions are that pressing. We work with toys, for God's sake. How immediate could any question be about them?

His arms folded across his chest, making his dark gray suitcoat rise up to reveal the open button on his white dress shirt, he leans against the doorframe and sighs. "Carey, before you go, I have to ask about the Rubik's cube display."

That's how he likes to frame questions that aren't really necessary.

As I slip my arms into the sleeves of my black sweater, I force myself to smile and say, "Okay. What can I do for you?"

What I really mean is closer to what can I say to make you go away.

Running his hands through his brown hair that desperately needs a trim, he narrows his dark eyes and stares like he's studying me. "I didn't see the six-sided version out there. I thought you said we received that for the display. It's important to have as many varieties as possible for guests to see. Do you know what happened to it?"

As his executive assistant and the person responsible for the social media for the museum, my job doesn't entail any kind of curating. He damn well knows I'm not the person responsible for what's included in any display.

So why ask me instead of Mrs. Carmichael, the curator who could answer his question? Because Monica Carmichael is a fifty-five-year-old woman who's worked here since they opened the doors of the Maryland Toy Museum in the early nineties, and she doesn't tolerate his idiotic questions for even a single second. Monica is the poster child for don't you dare waste my time, and you can always tell by the irritated look on her face whenever

Mr. James comes around her what she truly thinks of him.

"Mrs. Carmichael mentioned it had some issue that made it unacceptable to include in the display, Mr. James," I answer as sweetly as possible, already disgusted that it's got to be nearly five minutes after five on a Friday and he's keeping me here to talk about something that I have no control over.

Frowning, he draws his eyebrows in like two angry, black slashes but nods. "Okay. I'll have to ask her about that."

I keep smiling as I think that's exactly what he should have done in the first place. Back in the beginning right after I took this job, I thought it may have been possible he liked me and that's why he chose to constantly pester me with his idiotic questions. It would be juvenile, but I've never found that most men are that mature. I quickly decided he didn't think of me in any kind of romantic way since all I've ever seen in his expression whenever he's around me is mild irritation. He rarely looks pleased when he's near me. In fact, I'm pretty sure he doesn't even like me as a person.

That's why I never dare to tell him how much I don't appreciate him bothering me during non-work hours. I worry that would be all the reason he needs to fire me.

I begin moving toward the door, hoping he'll step aside so I don't have to squeeze past him once again. "Have a great weekend, Mr. James."

If I didn't dislike him, I might ask what he has planned since it's supposed to be a beautiful spring weekend with temperatures in the seventies for the first time this year. Since I don't feel that way about him, I leave it at my wish that he enjoy the next two days.

When I reach the doorway, he still hasn't moved, forcing me to stop in front of him. "Is there anything else? I'm late for my plans, so I really need to go."

Why he always has to make things so awkward between us I'll never understand. Normal people do not act like this toward their work subordinates, especially those they don't seem to like.

"No. I just wanted to know about that display," he says as he reluctantly steps out of my way. "But now that you mention it, did you post any pictures of that six-sided Rubik's cube?"

Mr. James, a man who I know for absolutely sure has never even seen a single post I've made in my job as social media coordinator since he abhors the very idea of social media and doesn't even have an account on any of the places I post pictures for the museum, stares into my eyes like he's sure he's going to catch me slacking off. He literally just has to go to the addresses I gave him when I made the accounts to check.

But no, he'd rather ask me at the very moment I want to leave for my well-deserved two days off. Maybe I should save the museum's accounts in his favorites so he never has to bother me again.

That won't work, though. He'll still ask me instead of checking for himself. Why, I have no idea.

I sigh, disgusted that it has to be nearly ten after five now. "Not yet. I did snap a few pictures, but I never post anything until I know it's been approved for the collection, Mr. James."

Why does he ask me questions like that? The man knows full well I only post about items people can actually find in the museum. I swear he does things like this just to be difficult.

He doesn't pick up on my utter disgust with him right now and nods his approval. "Very good. I'll check with Monica about that piece and get back to you about it."

"Okay. Have a nice weekend!" I repeat, choosing to be polite despite the fact that he's irritating as hell.

Even though I know he never wishes me a good weekend, I pause for the briefest of moments for him to say those nice words, but they never come. He simply stares as me strangely, as if he's sizing me up in some way.

Thanks for making it weird again, bossman.

I don't turn around as I hurry toward the door to leave, calling back as walk out into the hallway, "See you Monday!"

Even though I know he'll message or call me before then.

THE MOMENT I step outside into the warm sunlight, I close my eyes to enjoy the feeling of freedom on a beautiful spring afternoon. Taking a deep breath in, I inhale the sweet scent of the honeysuckle bushes some wonderful person planted long before I was born and silently thank them.

Sometimes on my lunch break, I'll come out here on warm days and sit at the old picnic table on the side lawn of the museum. Even though we're located in the middle of a city, it's surprisingly peaceful there.

Of course, that's until my boss comes loping over and wants to strike up a conversation about something work-related on what's supposed to be my break. That man has no understanding of personal boundaries.

My phone vibrates in the outer pocket on my purse, so I fish it out and see it's Emory calling. I wince as I remember she messaged before and I forgot to get back to her.

"Hey, I'm sorry," I say as I make my way to the staff parking lot on the side of the building. "I saw your text, but my boss came in, and you know how that goes."

My friend laughs like she always does when I mention Mr. James. "You're the only executive assistant I've ever heard of who has her own personal stalker. What is that guy's deal, Carey? Is he just working up to asking you out?"

I recoil in horror at that unsettling idea. "Uh, no, and I'll thank you to never utter those words again."

"So he's just an overbearing ass of a boss? I think you might be missing something right in front of your nose," Emory says, the lilt in her voice telling me she thinks this is funny.

A sound like footsteps behind me makes me suddenly nervous, so I spin around to look for whoever it is, but there's no one there. That's odd. I would have sworn when I looked there would be someone following me.

Mr. James, no doubt.

"Carey, are you there? Don't be mad. I'm just teasing you about that weird boss of yours."

My heart racing, I pick up my pace and hurry to my car a few yards away. "No, I'm fine. I'm not angry. I just thought I heard someone behind me, but when I turned around, no one was there."

"Maybe it was one of the toys. You know, I don't understand how you work in that place. That whole doll section creeps me the hell out. It's like every horrible doll nightmare I've ever had come to fruition right in that building. I bet at night they get up and terrorize the other toys."

I hate when she starts in on the doll thing. Of course, they freak me out. Who isn't uncomfortable with an entire room of dolls all staring blankly into space? One might be nice on a little girl's shelf, but hundreds? No, thanks.

"Please don't, okay? I just want to forget about work for the next two days."

As I reach my car, I hurriedly unlock the doors and throw my purse and tote bag onto the passenger seat before getting in behind the wheel. I don't know why I'm so unnerved right now. It's not like anyone was actually following me, and anyway, it's broad daylight, for God's sake. I'm just letting my imagination run away with me.

"I'm sorry, hon. I didn't mean anything. I was just teasing about the dolls. You know me. I have a doll problem. It's just a me thing. I'm sorry if I upset you."

I sit there in my car staring out the front window and listening to one of my best friends feeling bad for a second time in our conversation. God, I must sound like a real whiner today.

"You didn't. I think it's just been a long week. So let's start talking about whether or not we're going to try to see Jenna tonight. Do you think it'll be too busy at the restaurant for her to break away and hang out with us for a few minutes?"

That's not my real concern about tonight, but I don't want to bring that up.

"I talked to her at lunch, and she said she doesn't think it'll be too bad. She wants us to stop by. She said if we get there about eight, we should be able to get right in and she'll save her meal break until then so she can sit with us. It's going for five-thirty now. What do you say I pick you up at seven-thirty, or are you thinking you want to drive?"

Emory knows me well enough that on Fridays after a week of dealing with my boss I usually like to enjoy a drink or two when we go out. Tonight won't be any different either, so no driving for me.

"Seven-thirty is fine. I'm going to need at least a few martinis to take the edge off this week, so I'm happy to let you drive."

She doesn't drink, so this works best for both of us. Too many drunken nights in college ruined alcohol for her.

"Great! You want me to come up or just blow the horn?"

For a moment, my grandmother's criticism of every boy I dated in high school echoes in my head. Old-fashioned and from a different time, she insisted anyone I was going out with, male or female, had to come to the door to talk to her before I could leave the house. None of my female friends had a problem with it since they came over all the time, but every single boy balked at meeting my grandparents. She never relented, though, which meant hearing a lot of complaining from teenage boys just hoping to get into my pants. My grandmother knew that, though. I think she thought having to meet her and endure her grilling before I could leave would make them less interested in sex.

I never had the heart to tell her it didn't.

"Whichever you want," I say, sure Emory likely has no desire to walk up two flights of stairs to my apartment.

"Well, since I just upped my step count to fifteen thousand a day, I'll come up."

Fifteen thousand? I don't know how many I get, but I'd guess the total isn't even half that on my best days. No wonder Emory has such great legs.

Pushing my severely lacking physical fitness goals aside, I start my car and say, "Okay, seven-thirty. See you then!"

I set my phone in the cup holder on my console, put the car into drive, and gently press on the gas pedal, noticing my boss walking around the building. He doesn't have his briefcase, which means he's not leaving for the day, but something about the way he looks says he's searching for something.

Probably me. I better get out of here quickly, or if I know him, he'll be flagging me down and dragging me back into the building for some meaningless nonsense.

That man really needs to get a life.

3

The crowd at Remington's overflows out onto the sidewalk even though it's nearly eight-fifteen. Normally, the restaurant sees a slowdown after eight until nearly ten when the second wave of diners for the night arrive. Jenna may have been a bit too optimistic when she suggested we come by at eight o'clock.

Emory looks at me while she searches for a parking space in the crowded lot. "What's going on here tonight? Are they giving something away?"

I shrug, unsure why it's still so busy at this point in the evening. "We might not get to see Jenna after all. I'm wondering if we'll even get in."

Emory reaches over and gives my hand a gentle squeeze. "Don't worry. Everything's cool with us. Let's see if I can find a spot that won't require hiking blocks for our dinner."

We circle the lot three times before Emory finally spies someone pulling out of a space at the far end near the trees. In the daytime, that spot is almost like a park setting, but at night, it's more than a little eerie sometimes. For some reason, nobody designing the parking lot or the owners of the restaurant have ever thought to add a light to that area, so it's significantly darker than anywhere else on the property.

"How nice," Emory jokes as she drives into the spot and parks. "We get to park in the next state. I guess I shouldn't complain. It's just more steps, right?"

"Since I don't think I even get five thousand a day, I guess I can use the walk," I say with a chuckle as she turns off the engine.

"That's the spirit! You know, you should come walking with me. We could do it on your lunch break. It totally changes your attitude for the day. I used to hit a wall every day around two in the afternoon, but since I started walking a lot more, that's not happening anymore."

I turn to look at my friend and see she's serious. Leveling my gaze on her, I say, "Do I need to remind you about my work situation? I get a half hour lunch. I can use that to eat, or I can use that to walk, but I can't do both. I don't have the benefit of working from home."

A sheepish expression comes over her, and she gives me a half-hearted smile. "I'm sorry. I forgot about the half hour for lunch thing at the museum. I sound like one of those gung-ho gym assholes who thinks everyone has freedom in their schedule like I do. Just tell me to shut up the next time I do that, okay?"

"I get it, Emory. I wish I could walk more. I'm starting to think my bottom half is growing roots at my desk sometimes. Even if I had a longer lunchtime, you know my boss wouldn't let me go walking. He'd be following me like some silly fool asking me work questions the whole time."

We both laugh, but it's true. That boss of mine would be upping his steps too if I decided to walk on my lunch.

"Well, let's make the hike in there before the second rush arrives, although I'm pretty sure they're already here," she says as she opens her car door to get out.

"Do we have a plan for if we can't get in?" I ask as I follow her.

She looks up at the night sky and sighs. "Starve? Mickey D's? That diner we used to go to before Jenna got a job here and we started eating like adults?"

None of those sound appealing compared to Remington's food, so I hope the maître d' can find a place for us. I'm sure Jenna has told him we're coming, but if the restaurant is jammed, there won't be much he can do for us.

Emory slips her arm through mine while we walk toward the front door still blocked by a crowd of people. "Not to worry. I'm sure our good friend has hooked us up like she always does."

She's right. Jenna always takes care of us, so I'm sure I'm worrying about nothing.

Half an hour later after slowly carving our way through the group that had to number at least fifty people, we're seated at a table for three at the back of the restaurant overlooking the water, a view Remington's is famous for throughout the city. I see Jenna wave to us from the kitchen door and give us the sign she'll be over in five minutes.

I lower my menu and say to Emory, "I just saw Jenna. She'll join us soon."

Nodding, she says, "Cool. I'm thinking I want to try those mushroom things she's always raving about for an appetizer. By the way, did you see that guy with the dark hair on our way in? He was definitely liking what he saw with you."

She does that all the time, but I think it's mostly just an effort to try to boost my ego. Emory always claims guys are checking me out, but when I try to see who she means, there's not a soul looking in my direction.

I shake my head and smile, flattered that she's trying to be kind, but I'm not really ready to jump back into dating after my last relationship ended just two weeks ago. Better to be single for a little while and catch my breath.

Plus, I'm still not over Chase. My friends would think that's silly or sentimental, so I haven't mentioned how much I miss him. I'd rather them believe I'm as strong as they are and can't be bothered to think about him a second more in this lifetime.

"No, I didn't see Mr. Wonderful with the dark hair," I mumble from behind my menu.

A second later, Emory's hand forcibly lowers the menu, and she stares at me with a look full of judgment. "You know, it's okay to look even if you don't want to touch. You don't want to get out of practice."

"Out of practice? Of looking? I don't think I need to

practice the act of seeing, Emory. I think I mastered that a long time ago."

My friend screws her face into a harsh expression. "You know what I mean. You're in the prime of your life. You should be looking at men like they're your own personal smorgasbord."

Emory has never not seen men as delicious items on an endless menu she can choose from at any time. Committed to not settling down, she prefers to try the opposite sex like they're chocolates in one of those holiday sampler boxes.

I've never been very good at playing the field. I prefer to be monogamous, which to her is a fate worse than death. Maybe not death, but it's certainly far too boring for her to entertain for herself.

"I look," I say, hoping I don't sound too pathetic.

Her expression tells me I sound as sad as I wish I didn't. "When Jenna comes over, she's going to say the same thing, Carey. I know you were crazy about Chase, but you have every right to move on now that you two are over."

I hang my head, already tired of feeling sad about our breakup and unhappy Emory's already brought it up before dinner has even been served. "Please, could we not do this tonight? It's been a long week at work, and all I want to do is hang out with friends, have some good food, and enjoy a few drinks."

She gently touches my arm and lets out an audible sigh. "I'm sorry. I didn't mean to make you sad. Forget I said anything, okay?"

Nodding, I don't respond because I'm worried if I do, I

might tear up. My emotions are still too raw when it comes to Chase, especially since he hasn't stopped messaging me begging to come back. I don't answer him because I can't forgive much less forget he cheated on me.

"Did I miss something?" Jenna says in a cheery voice before she sits down across from me.

I look up and force a smile as I shake my head. "Nope. Well, other than Emory saying she wants to try the mushroom caps appetizer."

"Yes! Tonight's the night I finally take the plunge. I read mushrooms are good for the immune system, so it's time I come around to eating them. I also read they're good for strength, and I'm all about that these days," she says, flexing so we can see how lifting weights has given her really nice, muscular arms in her sleeveless dress. "My sculpting has become so much more refined now that I have more power in my hands and forearms."

Jenna throws her head back and laughs. "I don't think I'm ever going to get used to this Emory. To think your diet used to consist of fast food, various fried vegetables with dips, and enough beer to sink a ship."

Setting her menu on her plate, Emory puffs out her chest and grins. "Everyone has to grow up, but I'm glad I got all the bad stuff out of my system in my twenties. Now I'm focused on repairing the damage I did in my youth so I don't end up like my father with hardened arteries and diabetes before the age of fifty."

Jenna looks over at me and rolls her eyes. "In her youth. As if being in our thirties means we're old."

I've never felt old until this moment. It's probably just the way my life has been going lately. Thirty-two isn't old.

"You're quiet tonight," Jenna says, nudging my forearm. "What's going on?"

Shaking my head, I smile. "Nothing new. Same old, same old. Work at the museum and then home."

She looks across the table at Emory like they're exchanging some silent opinion about what I said, and then the two of them train their gazes on me. "Well, that's part of the reason I wanted you guys to come out tonight. You need to get back into it, Carey."

Although I'm curious about what the other part of the reason she wanted to see us is, I can't help but be a little snarky and ask, "Get back into what, Jenna?"

"Life!" Emory says far too loudly, making all the diners at the tables around ours turn and look at the three of us.

Jenna smacks her arm and in a low voice scolds her. "Hey, I have to work here. Let's try to behave like normal people for once."

That makes me chuckle, but my happiness is short-lived. It doesn't take long for both my friends to return their focus to me and my sad life. At least that's how they see it. I personally think I'm fine.

I'm just going through some things. It happens. I'll be fine once I get over mourning my breakup.

And I'd be a whole lot better if my friends could try to understand that.

"Seriously, honey. You need to get out of your funk," Emory says as she gives my hand a sympathetic squeeze like she's doing her best social worker impression.

I roll my eyes and turn to look at Jenna. "I guess it's

your turn. Go ahead then. Say what you have to say so we can order because I'm starving."

"We aren't trying to be bad friends, Carey. If anything, we're being good friends because we're worried about you. All you do is stay in your apartment night after night. You rarely go out anymore. Emory and I are just scared you're going to stay stuck in this spot you're in and never get out of it. That's all."

I love my friends, but right now, all I can think of is how I wish I was at my apartment they're so afraid I won't leave after tonight and not sitting here in a public place being examined to determine if I'm acting normally. How exactly is a person to act when they're heartbroken?

Not that I can say that to either of these women. Jenna is close to hating men entirely after her fiancé turned out to be a thief who stole all their savings meant for the wedding and ran off to somewhere in South America, and Emory sees relationships merely as efforts to stymie her freedom and efforts to be the healthiest version of herself.

Together, they view my interest in settling down with someone I love, getting married, and maybe having children as nothing short of ridiculous, each for their specific reasons. To say they're not the biggest cheerleaders for romance would be an understatement.

Even though I'm sure whatever I say will fall on deaf ears, I say it anyway, maybe for myself more than my friends. "I'm fine. Thank you for caring, but I'm good. Yes, I'm having a hard time getting over my breakup, but that's normal. Maybe not for either of you, but it is for me. Thank you, though."

That won't stop them from trying to pull me out of my funk, as Emory calls it, but at least I said my piece.

"We just worry about you. That's all," Jenna says in a voice that tells me it's more pity than concern. Then the manhating part of her rears its ugly head, and she adds, "Anyway, no man is worth even a tenth of the time you've given that ex of yours."

"Well, I'm fine. Can we order now? I'm starving," I say, forcing myself to smile to convince them to drop this whole thing, at least until I get some food in my stomach.

Thankfully, they believe my happy face, and a minute later, our server arrives to deliver our drinks and take our order. As I enjoy my lemon drop, Jenna and Emory busy themselves with discussing the proper eating habits of women our age, their conversation quickly dissolving into Jenna telling Emory the food she cooks is good for everyone and Emory complaining that there aren't enough vegetarian offerings on the menu. I quickly finish my first drink, pleased they're talking about anything but my situation.

AFTER PROMISING Jenna we'll do this again soon, Emory and I walk outside to see the crowd near the front door has only grown since we went inside to eat, so we have to weave through a line of people that stretches out into the parking lot. We make our way past a group of guys, which of course makes Emory ask if I like any of them. They smell like a mixture of pot and beer, and when one of them catcalls us, all I can do is roll my eyes at her and him.

"Oh, yeah. I'd like four of them. Maybe seven so I can have one for every day of the week."

Throwing her head back, she laughs at my attempt at being funny. "Fair enough. Let's go before I tell that guy exactly what I think of his offer."

Just before we reach the car, he yells, "Where you going? Stay here and let me show you a good time!"

Emory turns around and calls back, "You aren't big enough for either of these rides, baby. Stick to the kiddie rides!"

I look back and see him furious and beginning to storm toward us, so I bang on the roof of her car, getting more and more nervous with every step he takes. "Come on! Let me in this car before he gets here!"

She unlocks the doors just in time, and a few seconds later, she starts the engine. Our new best friend isn't done yet, though, and pounds his fists against her window. "Where you going? Let me show you how big I am!"

Emory looks over at me and grimaces. "Ick. Gross. Let's get out of here."

As she backs up, she lowers her window and yells out, "Fuck off, loser!"

She may think this is all funny and worthy of a hearty laugh, but all I can think is he's not going to give up now, even if we're driving away. I see him running after us and shake my head, unsure how a nice night out with my friends at a great restaurant turned into a scene from some high school drama.

When we exit the parking lot, I'm sure this is more

excitement than I've had in weeks, but Emory looks in her rearview mirror and says in disbelief, "Ridiculous! Do you know he's following us?"

I turn in my seat to look out the back window expecting to see him running behind us, but now he's driving his own car and actually tailing us. "Oh my God! What's he planning on doing? Running us off the road to prove we should want him? This is insane!"

My friend waves off my concern and laughs. "Not to worry. I'll lose this jackass."

Even as the question of what he intends on doing next fills my mind, she floors it and sails through a red light, barely missing a car coming through the intersection. "Ha! Beat that, loser!"

I look back again and see him still at the light. Relief fills me, and I sit back in the passenger seat, my stomach in knots after all the madness of the last few minutes. "Can't we just have a nice dinner out? You didn't have to egg him on like that, Emory. You know there's no winning with guys like that."

She shrugs as she turns onto my road, rolling her eyes. "He had all I said and more coming. Who the hell does he think he is pulling that kind of shit?"

Since I don't want to encourage her, I don't answer her question. He's just a drunk or stoned guy who thinks he's entitled to hit on women in his ugly way.

By the time she reaches my apartment complex, I'm eager to get inside and curl up with a nice cup of tea. Going out may be necessary, but all this excitement is more than I'm up for lately.

"Wait until I get inside to drive away, okay?" I say as I get out of the car.

"Why? Are you worried about that guy? He's long gone. I bet he's already back at the restaurant offending other unsuspecting women."

Leaning down, I give her my most serious look. "Just wait, okay?"

"Fine. Did you have a good time?" Emory asks with a chuckle.

"If being chased by a crazy man is a good time, then yeah. Drive safely, okay?"

Emory smiles. "I will. Hey, I say we get together next Friday. What do you think?"

I shake my head and sigh. "No can do. I have the museum benefit event next Friday."

"My apologies then. Sorry you have to spend time with that awful boss and others like him. I'll call you this week. Maybe we can do lunch."

"Sounds good! Now stay safe, and no more taunting other drivers. Do you hear me?"

Rolling her eyes, she puts the car in gear again. "Funny. I'll watch you until you get inside."

When I reach the glass front doors of my building, I turn around and wave goodbye to her before she drives away. I hurry inside and upstairs to my second floor apartment. When I close the door behind me, I can't explain why, but I immediately walk over to the window to look out.

My stomach drops when I see that guy's car slowly driving by my building. Did he follow us all the way from the restaurant, even after we thought we lost him at that red light? I didn't think he was that upset. Sure Emory said a few nasty things, but he had it coming. Why is he taking this so seriously?

Frightened, I yank the curtains closed and rush over to turn out the light in my living room. My hands shake as I make a beeline for my bed and decide not to wash my face before going to sleep or make a cup of tea. As I crawl under the covers and pull them up over my head, I wonder why things like this keep happening to me.

4

No sooner do I sit down at my desk on Monday, my boss strolls into my office like he's been waiting forever for me to arrive. He's likely been planning this conversation out the entire weekend, even though he texted me no less than ten times since he last saw me on Friday. Every single one could have waited.

Mr. James sits down on the edge of my desk and knocks over my framed picture of Garfield Jenna bought me to celebrate my starting this job. Then he shifts his weight and topples my pencil holder, sending pens and highlighters rolling all over the place.

Without even saying a word about the mess he's made, my boss launches into his questions he's waited to ask me, but I'm not listening. I'm too busy straightening up my work area, and at this moment, I don't care what he's saying.

"So I thought you'd have the list."

I jam the pens and highlighters into the black wire container and stand the picture up before looking up at him. God, I hope he can read the disgust in my expression.

"I'm sorry, Mr. James. I didn't quite get all of that."

He gives me a look of exasperation before sighing audibly. "Carey, this benefit is key to the museum being able to continue to run. I need to know you're one hundred percent involved in the preparations."

It takes channeling every ounce of calm inside me to not lash out at my boss for that ridiculous comment. I've been the one who's taken care of every last detail. I'm the person who made sure the invitations were corrected on time when he gave the printer the wrong information. I'm the only soul in this building who's completely dedicated herself to this museum fundraiser, and he thinks he should sit his fat ass on my desk, knock over all my knick-knacks, and spew his nonsense like he's the only person who cares about this event?

After taking a deep breath to give me a few seconds to remember how much I need this job, I plaster a smile on my face and say, "I can assure you, Mr. James, that I am doing all I can to make sure the benefit is a roaring success. I love this museum and want it to stay open."

Rarely have I said anything that emotional to my boss, so it's not surprising that he looks shocked when I finish. Better for him to feel that way instead of appalled by what I wanted to say.

He stands up from my desk, again knocking my Garfield picture over, and folds his arms across his chest. "Fine, fine. Very good. Have you spoken to the caterer yet today? It's the final day for menu changes, and I want them to know we must have canapes."

I want to scream because I'm the one who's reminded him for the past week about the deadline with the caterer, and every time he's practically ignored me. I'm going to get an ulcer from this job. I just know it.

"They don't answer their phones until ten in the morning, so I'll call them and make sure they know about the canapes then."

Mr. James looks at his watch and frowns. "What kind of business doesn't open until ten a.m.? That seems terribly unprofessional to me."

"They have to work events like ours that go well past the quitting time for those of us who work nine-to-five. I'm sure that's why their work schedule is as it is."

The flatness in my voice should indicate to my boss that he's overstayed his welcome in my office, but as usual, he doesn't take the hint. Instead, he walks over to the window that overlooks the grassy area on the side of the museum building.

"I wish we could have the event outside. I wonder if that's possible."

I stare straight ahead, my eye twitching, as I wonder if killing one's boss when you hear him express the desire to move the event you've worked on for three months is really a crime. Has he lost his mind, or is he just kidding?

Slowly, I turn around in my chair to face him. He looks like he's actually serious. I'm definitely getting an ulcer.

"Mr. James, the benefit has to be inside because we can't control the weather outside," I say as calmly as possible, overstating the obvious he should already know.

He nods and smiles, not knowing he's close to giving

me a heart attack. "That's right. Thank you, Carey. Well, it's almost ten, so I'll let you get going on that call to the caterers."

With that, he walks out of my office blissfully unaware he just casually mentioned upending the entire event. I swear to God I need to start playing the lottery so I might be able to quit this job before this man drives me out of my mind.

And as if my boss isn't enough to make this Monday a nightmare, just before I pick up the phone to call the caterers to finalize everything for Friday night, my ex-boyfriend texts me. Then he sends another message a minute later. And then another one.

Five minutes and ten texts later, I have a headache that threatens to blow the top of my head off. One glance at the messages and I see they all say the same thing every single one of his messages has said since the night we broke up.

Please forgive me. It meant nothing. I love you. You know we were good together.

On and on it goes with varying texts on those themes. Sometimes he says she meant nothing to me instead of it meant nothing. Those hurt the most. The others just make me wish I could change my phone number.

I don't respond to any of his messages, even though I could probably write a book with all I have to say to him. Giving him any answer at all will only encourage him, though, and I don't want that.

He slept with someone else. There's no coming back from that. I said those exact words the night I found out.

Nothing's changed since then. He can text me until he's blue in the face.

I don't care.

Except the problem is I do care, but I can't think about that now.

My phone vibrates for the eleventh time, and even though I know I shouldn't bother to look, for some reason this time my curiosity gets the better of me. One glance at his message and I know I made a mistake ignoring him.

You better start talking to me Carey or I'll come over to that job of yours and then everyone will hear our conversation.

That headache Mr. James created is mushrooming in size and taking over my entire head.

I wouldn't put it past my ex to show up here at the museum. He's run out of other options since I refuse to speak to him. The idea of that kind of humiliation in front of my coworkers is enough to make me think I should respond with something, but the last thing I want to do is make him think he's wearing me down.

He's not important now, though. I have work to do, and first on my list of things to accomplish is talking to the caterer. After that, I can figure out how to handle him.

FIFTEEN MINUTES LATER, I've reassured my boss that his canapes will be part of the food for the event and I'm outside in the beautiful sunshine to take my morning break. As much as I'd like to enjoy the few minutes away from my desk, I know I have to call my ex or risk him showing up here and making a scene.

He answers immediately, as if he's waiting by the phone for me. If only he had been that way when we were together and not sleeping with someone else, we wouldn't be broken up.

"Carey, I knew that threat about coming to your job would get you to call. I miss you."

What kind of love story do we have if the word threat has to be used?

"Chase, you can't keep doing this," I say as I begin to pace across the grass that seems particularly green this morning after the rain last night. "I'm at my work. I don't have time to be answering your texts and calls."

"Then come back to me, and you won't have to deal with them," he says in that cutesy voice I think I hate now even though I used to love it.

I take a deep breath in and exhale slowly, trying to find the right words to make him understand we're over. "That can't happen. You cheated on me. I can't forgive that. We have nothing else to talk about."

That sounds far stronger than I feel right now, but I can't buckle under the weight of my sadness at missing him. I just have to keep reminding myself of what he did to us.

"I'm not going to let you go, Carey. This isn't the end of us. I'm always going to be there. You're going to realize you want me like I want you. I just hope it isn't too late when you do."

Typical Chase. He starts out fine, but by the time he's

finished talking, he practically sounds like he's a stalker threatening my life.

"Goodbye. Don't call or text me again, okay? We're done. Finished. Go find that girl you slept with."

"I'm not giving up, Carey. We're not done. Not by a longshot."

"Yes, we are. You broke us, and that can't be fixed. Goodbye, Chase."

As I pull the phone away from my ear to end the call, I hear him say he's never going to let me go, so I better get used to it. What a sweet sentiment. The next thing I know, he'll be following me around like some sad puppy dog.

He calls three more times as I'm walking back to my desk, but I don't answer any of them. There's nothing more to say. All I can hope is he'll recognize that sooner than later.

So much for starting the week out on a good note.

As I settle in at my desk once more, I close my eyes and tell myself this isn't a problem. Yes, Chase can be difficult when he's not getting his way, but he's not used to us being over yet. He'll grow to understand it, and I bet he'll have a new girlfriend in no time. He's not ugly, and he has a good job, so I'm sure there are many women who would love to date him.

I smile at the last thought that crosses my mind before I open my eyes again. I'm just not one of those women anymore.

Not twenty seconds later, Mr. James walks into my office like a man on a mission. Assuming he's going to ask me something about the caterer for the tenth time this morning, I shuffle the papers on my desk so the contract the museum signed with them is right on top.

Before I can say a word to assure him his precious canapes will be on the menu, he sits down in front of my desk and leans forward toward me. He's only ever done anything like that when he wants to talk about another employee but doesn't want them to hear what he has to say. It's completely unprofessional, but I listen so just in case he's planning to fire anyone I'm friendly with here, I can give them some warning.

"Are you okay, Carey?" he asks with a sincerity I didn't expect.

I honestly don't know how to answer him. He doesn't want to know that his constant badgering makes my job incredibly challenging, so he definitely isn't asking if I'm okay with anything he's done. We don't talk about anything but work, which means his question has to do with something in our jobs.

But what I have no idea.

"I'm fine, Mr. James. I spoke to the caterer, and he made sure canapes will be offered to guests. I think that means we're all set for the event."

He nods as he hums his understanding or happiness. I'm not sure which, but either one works for me. As long as my boss is getting what he wants, he's actually quite pleasant to work with.

When he doesn't immediately stand to leave and instead continues to stare across the desk like he's studying me, I can't help but feel slightly unnerved. I want to ask if there's anything else he wants to discuss, but that will only open the door to his possibly piling on more work on top of the mountain of things I have to get done this week before the benefit.

"I'm glad you're okay. I saw you pacing back and forth outside on your break, so I was worried something might be wrong."

His statement confuses me for a few seconds. Was he watching me from his office window while I was outside on my break?

I want to believe that he's being kind by showing concern for my well-being, but in my mind, red flags are popping up everywhere. Does he make it a habit to watch me when I'm outside? I take my breaks outside the building whenever it's nice. Is he watching me every time?

Unsure how to answer him, I force a smile and shake my head. "Oh, I'm fine. Nothing to worry about. I better get back to work on the last-minute details for the benefit."

"Yes, yes. That's a good idea for me too. I'm happy to hear there's nothing wrong, Carey. Okay, I'm off to meet with the trustees at the annual meeting this afternoon. Let me know if anything comes up that I should know about."

Nodding, I watch him stroll out of my office, finally leaving me to my work, but all I can think about now is he's watching me. But why?

5

Private Message

You think your life is safe and secure, just like most people do. They go along with their daily lives not paying attention to details that could mean the difference between life and death and fixating on nonsense they see on social media or on their favorite TV series.

It's a mistake, but you rarely notice it until it's too late.

You never know how people see you either. It's been said every person in the world sees you differently, that for each person there's a version of you. So that day when you weren't nice to the checkout girl at the grocery store because you were having a hard time at work, she saw you as a villain. You were someone who made her life worse for those few brief moments you two were together at the register.

Then she told her friends about you, and maybe one of them recognized her description of your face with those big blue eyes or your long, straight blond hair. Just that one interaction with that girl at the store then changes another person's opinion about you, and suddenly, there are two people who think you're a villain.

See, that's how it is. You may think you're one of the sweetest people on the planet, but not everyone sees that in you.

But that checkout girl isn't going to do anything about how she feels. The anger at you will pass, and maybe if she sees you another time and you're pleasant, she'll forget how terrible you made her feel that one time.

The human brain is capable of amazing things, but strangely enough, holding memories about emotions isn't one of them. Everyone says they're never going to forget in the moment. They rant and rave about some person or event that infuriates them, and then some time goes by, and they don't truly remember how awful they felt. Sure, the memory remains, but the emotions attached to that memory fade into nothingness.

That's why people are so absolutely sure nobody would ever want to do them harm. How could they? What have you done to make anyone hurt you? You're always so kind and considerate.

Except for that time at the store. And when you were super hungry that day at lunch and were rude to the person standing behind you in line at the fast food place. Or that night you didn't feel like you needed to be polite to that drunk who yelled at you from across the parking lot.

You assume you're a good person, but are you really?

It seems to be an impossible thing managing all the

different ways people see you. How can you account for what you make someone feel? It actually seems quite wrong to blame that on you. "That's their problem," you say to yourself. You can't truly be responsible for how others see you. To expect that of anyone is an impossible task.

But that's the problem, isn't it? You can't know what's going on in someone's life on that day when you walk into it. Did their husband or wife leave them, and then you appear and you remind them of that person they lost? Did their boss just give them the bad news that they're losing their job, and then you run into them when they're feeling their lowest?

You can't know. Oh, sure you can do your best to be civil to strangers, but what if that's not enough? What if giving that person a smile today is the sign they need that it's time to finally show the world they demand more than fake politeness?

Nobody can truly know what's happening in another person's life. That smile you gave that's hiding the sadness you feel may be interpreted as smugness or indifference.

You see, it's all so dangerous because you can't see what others are really feeling.

Have you ever seen a news story about someone who snapped one day? They were living their life, and then something set them off and they lost it. They lash out by gunning down perfect strangers or attacking someone on the street, and all those people who knew the victims wonder why.

Why that wonderful person who was always so kind?

Why that quiet person who never bothered anyone? Was it simply a matter of being in the wrong place at the wrong time?

You want to believe that's the case. That bad things randomly happen with no cause other than a person happened to be somewhere they shouldn't have been. That sense of chance, while it bothers many who prefer more concrete answers, actually can make you feel better about things. It wasn't anything personal. It was just something that happened. No one meant to hurt them.

Then again, that's not always the case. Sometimes it's intensely personal.

You think no one is paying attention because you're just the low man on the totem pole. You're not the boss. You're not the person in charge. You're merely a cog in a much bigger wheel with far more important people making decisions.

And you like your life that way. It makes you feel like you have no responsibility for the truly difficult things that happen in your life.

The problem is that false sense of security makes you feel like you're not in danger. Why would anyone care about someone so insignificant? You're just one person in a world of people. No one notices you. You're simply little old you.

But I see you. I see you when you're on your way to work. I see you when you walk outside on beautiful, sunny days to have your lunch or take your break. I see you out with your friends. I see you at the supermarket.

I see everything you do.

The most interesting thing to me is you never notice

me. The real me. Not that I'm trying to have you see me. Not yet. I'm happy to remain in the background of your world.

But one day soon, you'll see who I really am.

Until next time, Carey...

6

Guests begin to file in through the museum's front door, and I watch for their reaction to the way the party planner decorated everything in shades of blue and gold. I wasn't sure those were the best colors for the event, but Mallory swore they would be stunning.

I guess she was right.

My boss buzzes around greeting people like the host with the most, but as much as he irritates me, I know he cares dearly about the museum like I do so I applaud his efforts like tonight. I watch him smile at each guest and imagine his cheek muscles must be hurting since I don't think Mr. James smiles even once a day when he's at work.

Next to me, Mallory the party planner taps on my shoulder, and when I turn to look at her, she's all smiles too. "I told you the color scheme would work. I'm off to celebrate yet another stunning achievement in design. I'll be looking on the socials for pics. Have a nice night!"

Before I can ask her if she'd like to stay to toast her

work, she sails off through the crowd toward the door, leaving me standing near the champagne fountain all by myself. That's okay, though. I leave the schmoozing to Mr. James. I'm better at the one-on-one types of interactions, which I don't expect to encounter much of tonight.

"This is a great party," a deep voice says behind me.

I turn around and see a man dressed in a tux with light brown hair and a tan that makes him look like he belongs at the beach. Instantly, I'm drawn to his deep green eyes. He's attractive but something about him makes me think I've seen him before, although I can't imagine where. We definitely do not look like we travel in the same circles.

"I'm happy you're enjoying yourself," I say with a smile. "The more attention we can get for the museum, the more we can do here."

His eyes open wide like he's surprised, and I can't help but notice the yellow flecks around his pupils. They threaten to change the brown in his eyes to a gold shade I've never seen before.

"So you work here? How is it my friend has never told me about someone so lovely working with him?" the man asks in a very flirtatious tone.

I'm flattered but unsure which of my coworkers could be his friend. "I do. I'm an assistant to the director of the museum. I also handle all the museum's social media."

The man's gaze moves toward my boss and then he nods. "Randall has been keeping you a secret. Every time I see him out in public, he talks about this museum of his nonstop, yet never once has he told me his assistant was so beautiful."

Extending his hand to shake mine, he finally introduces himself. "I'm Nicholas Madera. It's very nice to meet you."

"Carey Mitchell. It's nice to meet you, Nicholas."

His skin is soft against mine, although his handshake is almost too firm, gripping my hand just a shade too tightly. Thankfully, he releases his hold on me quickly to get me a glass of champagne.

"I think it's only right we toast our auspicious meeting tonight. When Randall practically badgered me to attend this event tonight, I said yes but was convinced it would be another boring night full of old people who smell like mothballs and bad cologne. To say I'm happily surprised would be an understatement."

His description of what he anticipated tonight would be like may not be complimentary, but he's not too far off with it. I think the scents he's thinking of are from the fur coats the older, very wealthy women take out of storage for these kinds of events, along with the aftershave some of the elderly men splash on a little too liberally. I guess I've just never thought about them the way Nicholas does.

I feel like I need to defend the people he's just insulted, albeit amusingly, so as I take the flute of champagne from him, I say, "The museum would be lost without all these wonderful supporters and donors, you know. It's very hard to get people to support places like this that focus on less well-known parts of American history."

Nicholas doesn't respond for a moment and simply stares at me before saying, "Beautiful and diplomatic.

Very admirable. Don't worry, Carey. These people wouldn't care if they heard me talking about them like I did. All they care about is money, and since I have enough to buy and sell them, they'll take whatever I say, complimentary or not. But let's forget them and focus on what's important. To meeting new people at events we're forced to attend."

I watch him clink his glass off of mine and repeat a portion of his toast. "To meeting new people."

Since I hadn't thought I'd meet anyone at tonight's benefit because it's usually only those older people he just described, I instantly wish I had chosen the sexier red dress instead of the black dress I always wear to these things. It's short, like the red one, but it's got nothing interesting about it, so I think I usually just blend in with the scenery whenever I wear it. That was fine when I thought I was attending this to fulfill my job responsibilities, but now that I'm talking to a good looking man close to my age, I'm sure the red dress would have been a better choice.

"You got quiet there," he says, stepping in front of me so I can't see the people walking into the event.

Focusing on his face and those very unique eyes of his, I shake my head. "No, just thinking about my choice of outfit tonight. Silly, actually. I do have to admit I wish women had a go-to look like men do with tuxes."

I sound like a rambling idiot, so I stop myself and take a drink of champagne. Nicholas studies me for a long moment before letting his gaze travel up and down my body. I guess I could be insulted since he's so obviously checking me out, but after I introduced the topic of what

I'm wearing tonight, it feels a bit hypocritical to be upset he's actually looking at my dress.

"I think what you chose is perfect for this event. To be honest, I'm a little surprised to hear you had a choice in the matter. Randall likes to choreograph things like tonight down to the tiniest detail, so I would have thought he'd have told you what to wear."

Without thinking, I laugh and say, "He likes to dictate a lot of things around here, but my clothes don't seem to be on that list yet."

Instantly, I regret every word of that sentence, so I quickly add, "Not that he's a terrible boss or anything like that. Mr. James is a wonderful person to work with. For. With."

Oh, God. I really am rambling. There's no stuffing the genie back into the bottle now. He's going to repeat what I said to my boss, and then I have no idea what's going to happen, but it certainly won't be good.

Nicholas gently sets his hand on my arm and smiles. "Don't worry. I won't tell him you think he's a tin-plated dictator. Not that he doesn't know that already. Trust me. Everyone he knows has called him that at one point or another."

None of that makes me feel better. Whoever those people are, they have the means to tell Mr. James whatever they want. I, on the other hand, need my job. I don't have the luxury of insulting the man who determines how much raise I get or if I even get to keep working here.

"Please don't say a thing to him," I whisper. "I love working at the museum. I'd hate to lose my job."

Oddly, my genuine fear at being unemployed after

tonight doesn't worry him, and he waves my concern away. "Nonsense. If he was ever stupid enough to fire someone like you, I'd hire you in a second and I'd guess at twice the amount you're getting paid here. He knows that, so he won't be letting you go anytime soon. Trust me on this. I have no doubt he likes working with you too much."

Something about the way he says that hits my ears wrong. Does my boss tell his friends he enjoys having me working here? Why? It's not like we're close. We certainly aren't friendly. In fact, if anything, he's overbearing and rarely seems pleased by my work.

I sputter out something that makes it seem like I'm flattered by his saying Mr. James likes working with me, but what I'm really feeling is a little creeped out. I'm probably just overreacting to earlier in the week when my boss admitted he was watching me while I was outside having that terrible conversation with my ex. Whatever aggravation my boss causes me, he couldn't hurt a fly.

"Okay, enough talk about your work. Tell me something else about yourself."

Never before have I heard anyone demand something in such a pleasing voice. I waste a few seconds taking a sip of my champagne while I frantically try to think of something to tell him that would sound interesting. Unfortunately, my working at a toy museum is honestly the most interesting thing about me, although I don't know what that says.

Unable to think of anything but that one odd ability I

possess, I answer, "I can sleep standing up like horses do."

In the entire history of mankind, no sentence has been uttered that is less sexy. A good looking man with money and confidence, two things I don't tend to attract much in the opposite sex, wants to know about me, and I tell him the most bizarre trait I can think of.

And I wonder why I'm single.

Nicholas doesn't miss a beat and says, "I've never heard anyone say that. I think you might be the most interesting person I've ever met."

"That's nice of you to say, but you can be honest. It's weird. I know. For what it's worth, I rarely actually fall asleep standing up. I try to be lying down when I get tired."

With every word that leaves my mouth, I'm sure I'm making things worse, but Nicholas continues to smile and nod as he listens to every peculiar syllable I utter. I should just stop. There are dozens of other topics we could be discussing, particularly considering we're in a toy museum that houses a fair number of unique items.

However, he seems interested in continuing this conversation and asks, "How did you find out you could sleep standing up? Was it just something that happened one day when you were standing in line for a long time?"

And just like that, I have to admit something even more awkward. I down the rest of my glass of champagne and answer, "No, my mother realized it when I was young. She was worried I had narcolepsy, but thankfully, it turned out I'm simply weird."

He thinks I'm being self-effacing and brushes his hand against my arm, a sign he also thinks my idiocy is charming. If I had known men enjoyed hearing such ridiculous things about a woman, I would have mentioned that little quirk in my personality ages ago instead of keeping it hidden.

Leaning in as a couple walk near us to reach the champagne fountain, Nicholas whispers in my ear, "Since we're sharing things, here's one for you about me. I routinely confuse narcolepsy with necrophilia. I have no idea why."

I turn to look at him and see honesty written all over his face. I can't remember when, if ever, someone mentioned necrophilia in a casual conversation, but I have to admit by doing that, he's put me more at ease.

"You know, I think if anyone heard our conversation, they'd think we're strange," I say with a tiny laugh.

He leans in even closer so I can feel his tux jacket brush against my cheek. "There's nothing wrong with strange, don't you think?"

The smell of his cologne fills my nose with hints of musk and something woodsy, a potent combination of scents that make it hard for me to think straight. I want to say something clever, but I can't seem to come up with anything even coherent.

My boss comes around the champagne fountain and stops abruptly when he sees Nicholas and me talking. Wearing an expression of utter shock, he first looks in my direction like he wants to reprimand me and then turns his focus to his friend.

"Madera! I was wondering where you were. I have

some people I know you're going to want to meet. They're waiting over there. Come on."

The way he completely ignores me should make me angry, but I'm just happy to not be the focus of his attention for once. When Nicholas doesn't respond, that's when Mr. James turns his head to look at me, and as usual, he looks unhappy.

"Carey, I saw the waiters with canapes, but that's the only appetizer I've seen floating around so far. You did make it clear to the caterers that canapes were only supposed to be one of the choices and not the only choice, didn't you?"

I'm embarrassed he's chosen this very moment to treat me like a moron, and all I want to do is lash out at him. I don't, though. As always, I can't forget I need this job, so I take what he dishes out, even if I want to scream.

"Yes, Mr. James. I made sure to tell them to add the canapes, not substitute them for all the usual appetizers," I answer with a fake smile, making sure my tone indicates how stupid he sounded when he asked me his question.

I expect him to march away with Nicholas in tow, but my new friend speaks up to defend me. "Randall, this woman is quite capable, obviously. You've told me yourself how well your employees handle their jobs. Why do you have to talk to her like she's the village idiot? I saw other appetizers floating around, as you say, before I walked over here to talk to Carey."

My mouth drops open, but I quickly close it so I don't look as stupid as my boss tried to make me seem. Mr. James shoots Nicholas a nasty glare before turning on his heel and marching away, leaving the two of us alone once more.

"Thank you," I say as I take another flute of champagne. "You didn't have to stand up for me, but I appreciate it. Mr. James just gets—"

Nicholas cuts me off before I can say something to defend my boss. "He gets overzealous and should be told off. That whole thing he did wasn't okay, and I plan on telling him what a giant bore he was saying that in front of me."

I hate that our time together has been ruined by my boss and his ridiculous need to dress me down. Hanging my head, I quietly say, "You don't have to do that. In fact, it would be better if you didn't. I need this job."

"Trust me. He won't fire you. I told you. He likes having you around too much. And if he's dumber than I think, you can always come work for me."

Smiling, I lift my head. "Do you have a museum director who needs an executive assistant?"

"No, but I have hundreds of people who work for me, and I'm sure one of them is getting ready to resign as we speak. You give the word, and I'll have you set up in a job faster than you can tell Randall what he can do with this job and his bullshit behavior."

He has no idea how much I appreciate that, even if it is probably just a way to flirt with me. I tolerate much of what Mr. James does during our hours together in this building because I can't afford to lose my job. Knowing I might have one with whatever company Nicholas owns eases my worries a little.

"Thank you. Mr. James is okay. He's just wound a little tightly when it comes to the museum."

Nicholas rolls his eyes. "You're far too diplomatic. I would have told him where he could stick that attitude of his if he spoke to me like that."

"That's because you don't have to worry about losing your job."

He doesn't say anything to that but reaches into his tux jacket and pulls out a pen and paper, handing them to me. "I'd love to see you sometime when we aren't surrounded by mothball and Old Spice people. Write down your number before Randall comes back and drags me over to whoever he wants me to meet. I know him. His feelings will mend quickly, so we don't have much time."

Although I don't know anything about Nicholas other than his name, I do as he asks and give him my phone number. Mr. James marches toward us as I hand the pen and paper back to Nicholas, and he stuffs everything inside his coat just as my boss is rounding the fountain.

"Thank you for not mentioning how old-fashioned it is to write things down," Nicholas says with a chuckle. "I'm old school. Now if you will excuse me, my friend is going to insist I come with him this time. I'll keep him occupied for as long as possible, so go grab some of those all-important canapes and enjoy yourself for a while."

He barely gets that last word out before Mr. James stops in front of him, arms folded across his chest to show his unhappiness that his friend is still talking to me. "Carey has a list of things a mile long she needs to handle, so I'm going to have to insist you come with me, Nick."

Turning to look at me, Nicholas says, "See? I told you. Insists. It's all this guy ever does. I'll speak to you soon, Carey."

My boss throws me a nasty look like I'm detaining his friend when he truly wants to be somewhere else and then leads Nicholas away. He glances back at me once on his way over to whatever people Mr. James needs him to speak to and winks, and all I want to do is look around to see if that was meant for me.

It's not every day good looking men with money are interested in me. Jenna and Emory? Sure. Not me, though.

I can say it's a nice change, though.

7

THE BENEFIT GOES off without a hitch, and by the end of the night, all I want to do is go home to bed. Nicholas disappeared after my boss dragged him away to talk to someone, leaving me to myself for a while. Mr. James found me less than a half hour later, though, worried about people putting their champagne glasses on the display cases and leaving marks. If it's not one thing with that man, it's another.

Isn't it enough that people came out in support of the museum and pledged money so we can offer even more interesting exhibits? Aren't a few marks on the glass display cases worth that? Those water marks are proof that they bothered to tour the museum and stopped to look at what we offer instead of just staying put near the champagne fountain. Of course, he wouldn't see it like that.

As he was complaining about such a trivial matter, I wanted to hold up my phone in front of his face and show him all the great pictures I took to post to social media.

The turnout tonight is such a wonderful testament to all we've accomplished here at the museum. I didn't, though. Mr. James doesn't appreciate social media in the least.

I wander around the collection rooms looking for stray champagne glasses so my boss doesn't have a meltdown if he sees one. Contrary to what he said in that frantic tone earlier, I only find one in the preschool toy room sitting on the case holding See and Says and coloring books.

As I'm rubbing the water stain away, he comes up behind me and exclaims, "See! I swear people don't understand what such careless attitudes can do."

I turn around and can't help but be disappointed to see him alone. "It's okay, Mr. James. I cleaned off the glass, and now it's as good as new. Nobody will be the wiser. Now I'm just going to find the caterers so I can return their champagne flute."

Taking a step around him, I try to leave, but he stops me, grabbing my arm. My boss has never touched me in any way, which is how I would have preferred to keep our relationship, if I'm being honest, and the feel of his hand on my bicep unnerves me.

I stare him down, something that ordinarily tells people to stop whatever they're doing and change course, but he doesn't let go of me. When I open my mouth to tell him I need to leave, he shakes his head, confusing me.

"Nicholas Madera isn't the usual kind of man you associate with, I'm going to assume."

As I often do when my boss talks to me, I take a few moments to think about what he's said. This time, all I want to do is yank my arm from his hold and tell him it's none of his damn business what kind of men I associate with.

I don't, though. Despite knowing that Nicholas said I would have a job if Mr. James is stupid enough to fire me, I like working at this museum, so I simply remain silent.

"Be careful, Carey. That's all I wanted to say."

With that, he lets go of my arm and hurries out of the preschool room, leaving me utterly baffled by his comment. Be careful? Of what? Is he referring to his friend? Who says that kind of thing about a friend? Is there something I should know about Nicholas?

I'd assumed my boss's comment about not usually associating with men like Nicholas referred to his wealth and my lack of it. Did he mean something else? If so, giving me some cryptic warning and then rushing off wasn't helpful at all.

With all that filling my head, I look around the museum to ask him to explain what he meant, but I can't find him anywhere. I poke my head into each collection room with no luck. Where could he be? He never bolts right after one of these events. He's obsessive about staying until the final person in the building leaves.

Wouldn't you know it? The one time I actually want to talk to him, he's nowhere to be found.

After finding his office door closed and the room dark, I search a few more places in the building before giving up and walking into the kitchen area where the caterers are packing up. "Has anyone seen Mr. James?"

Every head turns and eight people stare at me for a few seconds before they all answer no. How is that possible? The man makes a pest out of himself at every one of these events. I've heard the catering staff complain about him giving them a hard time after every benefit we've held here.

Now suddenly, he's practically disappeared into thin air after dropping that baffling bit of advice on me?

Twenty minutes later, I've made sure the museum is cleaned up and ready for visitors tomorrow, so I thank the catering staff and make my way to my car. It's the only one left in the employees' parking area, like some sad orphan somebody left behind in the darkness.

"I should have parked in the front," I mumble as I walk across the parking lot flanked by trees that only serve to make things even darker.

My mind begins to conjure up fearful ideas of someone hiding in the brush and attacking me as I look for my keys, so I quickly fish them out of my purse and hold them between my fingers like that woman from the self-defense course last year told us to do. Not that I think I could injure anyone like this. It seems like a good idea until you realize it would take the strength of a linebacker to thrust a key into someone's skin. I'd be lucky to even draw blood.

"You're fine," I whisper into the darkness. "Nobody is out to get you here."

As much as I wish that would calm my nerves, it does nothing as I pick up the pace and racewalk toward my car. The single streetlight is too far away to illuminate anything near my parking spot, and I think to myself that I need to bring up to my boss the next time I see him that we need at least one more out here.

The sound of footsteps behind me makes the hair on

the back of my neck stand up straight. I want to turn around to see if I'm hearing things or if there's actually someone there, but I'm too afraid.

What was that thing the self-defense woman said to do if you want to scare someone away? Oh, God! I knew I should have paid more attention to her, but she had such a hippy-dippy thing going on that I had a hard time taking her seriously.

I hurriedly try to remember that technique. What did she call it? Something about shock and awe, I think, but how am I supposed to do that? Damnit, I'm going to end up dead because I was scrolling through social media at the very moment I should have been paying attention to her.

Another noise like a footstep landing on a twig on the pavement makes every muscle in my body go stiff. Please let me remember that shock and awe thing.

Then, in a flash, it all comes back to me, and I remember what she said. "Press the alarm button on your car's key fob. It will scare anyone following you, and most of the time, it will give you at least a chance to reach your car and lock the doors."

Thank you, hippy lady!

I do as she instructed, making my car alarm begin to screech like some wild animal being attacked. My headlights flash on and off, adding to the jarring effect. I don't turn around to see if all of this terrifies anyone, instead hurrying over to my car to get to safety.

When I'm safely inside, I turn off the alarm and lock the doors before I let out a heavy sigh of relief. I have no idea if anyone was actually following me, but now as I sit in the darkness of my car, I'm thankful that I can at least remember that technique from the self-defense course Jenna insisted we all take.

I bet there was no one there. I do this all the time. I let my mind run away with me, and before I know it, I'm convinced I'm going to be murdered walking to my car. Seriously, what are the chances of that?

Sure it was all in my head, I start my car and drive out of the parking lot. I see no one anywhere around, which tells me I let my imagination get the best of me again.

AFTER A QUICK SHOWER TO wash away a full workday and a few hours of extra work at the benefit, I crawl into bed to fall asleep, exhausted from all the excitement of the day. As I close my eyes, I think about Nicholas and wonder if he'll actually call. He seemed genuine when he asked for my number, so I want to believe he will.

My boss's odd warning echoes in my head as I think about my time with Nicholas tonight, but I push it away, refusing to listen to Mr. James when it comes to my love life. The man dictates every move I make from nine to five, Monday through Friday, but when it comes to my free time, he can keep his opinion to himself.

Feeling rather pleased with how the night went and my tiny declaration of independence, I begin to drift off to sleep. Suddenly, I'm jolted awake by the realization that I forgot to put out my garbage. I silently debate whether it'll be okay if I wait until the morning or if I need to get dressed and take it down to the bins now, and

I sadly decide I can't wait until I wake up. If I do, the whole apartment will stink.

Irritated I have to get out of bed, I grumble about how I wish I had the concierge service Emory gets at her apartment complex. Every night, someone comes around and picks up her trash right outside her front door. She also pays five hundred dollars more a month than I do, which isn't something I can manage right now.

So downstairs with garbage bag in hand I go.

By the time I slip into a pair of shorts and a T-shirt, I'm doing the math in my head to see if I really can't afford to move to where Emory lives. In addition to the concierge trash pickup, she also has a gorgeous workout area and a pool, neither of which my complex has. I have been meaning to get back into exercising, so it would be good to have that gym right on site.

None of that changes the fact that my job at the toy museum doesn't pay enough for me to afford a place with all those perks. Still, it would be nice.

I walk down the stairs to the first floor where everyone in my building leaves their trash and toss the bag in with all the others, noticing there have to be twice as many garbage bags this week compared to every other time. Then I remember Mrs. Alcott had her retirement party on Thursday. All those people from her job at the high school made a lot of trash.

As I trudge down the sidewalk toward the stairwell, I hear something that sounds like footsteps again. Am I losing my mind? Twice in one night seems a bit strange to think someone's following you.

This time, I look around, but I see no one. Across the

parking lot, I see that family that lives on the first floor of the south building still has every light in their apartment on. That's probably what I was hearing. Their teenage sons are always milling about at all hours of the day and night. It's likely them I'm sensing.

That's it, I'm sure.

I hurry back up the stairs, repeating in my mind that it's those teenagers and nothing more, but I can't help but feel uneasy. When I stop on the second floor and look out at the parking lot, I have the surest feeling someone's out there watching me.

"This is an apartment complex, Carey. You live around hundreds of other people. Of course, there's someone seeing you. How many times have you watched one of your neighbors when they walked down to the dumpster or strolled along the sidewalk with their dog?" I mumble to myself before turning to head back to my apartment.

I really need to stop letting my imagination run away with me. Nobody is that interested in me or my life to spend time following me.

Well, other than my ex, but he's not the type to keep to the shadows. If he was here, he'd be front and center trying to talk me into taking him back. He's definitely not a man who ever does anything without everyone knowing.

I'm just being silly. Nobody's following me or spying on me. I'm simply not someone that ever would happen to.

8

AT FIVE AFTER nine on Monday morning, I notice the door to my office is closed, so I jump up and hurry over to open it, knowing my boss will read me the riot act if he sees that. Mr. James always says that closed doors in an office indicates a closed mind, and he won't have either in his building.

He has pithy sayings like that for dozens of things that happen on the job. They seem to be his version of Chinese fortune cookies. I always smile and nod when he launches into one of his dissertations on those hot button issues of his. I made the mistake of asking him about the door having to be open when I was new at this job, and I had to listen to half an hour of explanation of the psychology of what a closed door means. Since then, whenever he feels the need to lecture on anything he sees as important, I just nod like I'm listening and smile every so often to make it seem like I agree with him.

By half past nine, I'm surprised he hasn't come to see me yet this morning. Mr. James always starts his workday by visiting my office to remind me of something I've written down on my calendar. He knows that, but he claims he has OCD, so he can't help himself from bringing things up repeatedly.

I think he has the disease that makes him a PITA. If just once he could acknowledge the fact that I've never forgotten a single thing he needed me to remember, I think I could die a happy woman.

Since that's not going to happen, I guess I'll have to find my happiness elsewhere.

Leaning over toward my office window, I look out at the employee parking lot to check if he's arrived yet. That's strange. His car isn't in the special parking spot designated for the director of the museum located at the end of the front row of spaces mostly reserved for drivers who are handicapped. That's very odd, but it's also good because it means I can relax and enjoy myself at work for one of the few times since I took this job.

I grab my phone and call Emory since out of all of my friends, she's the only one I know I won't be interrupting at just after nine a.m. Jenna is surely still fast asleep after a night of working at the restaurant, and everyone else I know is already settled in at their jobs by this time of day.

"Carey, what's wrong?" Emory asks before I get a chance to say hello.

"Why would something be wrong?" I ask, utterly confused at how this conversation has begun.

"You're calling me on a Monday morning while you're at work. You've told me all about your boss, and I know he can't be okay with you calling your friends on the museum's dime."

Now You Know How It Feels 71

Her explanation makes me laugh. "Good to know my friends pay attention when I complain about my job. Mr. James isn't here yet, so I figured I'd take advantage of that far too rare anomaly to call you."

Emory lets out an audible sigh into the phone. "Whew. I was worried something bad had happened. So where is Mr. Uptight on this fine Monday morning? I wonder if he's sleeping in and being lazy. They're going to take away his overachiever card for this."

"I can't imagine my boss doing either. I'm sure he's just stuck in traffic or at a dentist appointment or something like that. It would be too much to ask to get a whole day without him hovering over me like some helicopter parent."

As I finish saying that, a noise outside in the hallway makes my heart skip a beat. If Mr. James heard that, I can kiss my yearly raise goodbye. He's the type of person who never forgets a slight.

Emory chatters on about something as I hold my breath, expecting to see him poke his head in and grimace at me. That doesn't happen, though, and after a few seconds more, I return to paying attention to what my friend is saying.

"...and since it's such a beautiful day out, and I'm not working today, I thought I'd come down to see you."

Confused since Emory rarely visits me at my work, I ask, "Do you mean today?"

"Weren't you listening? I'm having an awful day with my muse. I've been up since six, but I can't get a thing to come to me, so I figured I'd drive down to see you at the museum. I'll bring lunch, and we can sit outside in that nice grassy area with picnic tables on the side of the building where we hung out that day last summer with Jenna. They didn't get rid of those cute little tables, did they?"

"No. School kids use them when they eat lunch after touring the museum."

Laughing, Emory asks, "Well, are you inundated with rugrats today, or will we be able to eat our lunch in peace?"

"As far as I know, we'll be fine. I'm just surprised to hear you want to come here to have lunch. You haven't been to my job since last summer."

"Well, today seems like a good day to rectify that. What time do you eat lunch?"

I glance at the clock on my laptop and see it's going for ten o'clock. "In about two hours I should be able to take my lunch. It might be later, though, once my boss gets here. He'll come in late and then want to fit an entire day of work in."

Emory groans. "I don't know how you put up with him, Carey. I'd want to strangle that man if I had to work with him."

As always, my immediate reaction to anything anyone says about my boss is to defend him. I don't know why. I've had that very same thought at least half a dozen times, so why should I care if someone else says it?

"He's not so bad. He's just very serious about his job. I can't fault him for that."

"Well, forget about him. I'll be there at noon, and if he gives you a hard time taking your lunch break, I'll give him a few words of advice. See you in a little while!"

I barely have enough time to turn around and get back to my work on my laptop before the assistant director of the museum knocks on my office door. Younger than my boss, Michael Tanner is the polar opposite of Mr. James. Not only is he at least six inches taller than my boss, but he's also far more attractive with light brown hair and blue eyes I swear look like actual sapphires. Friendly, he always has a smile for everyone, and I know his assistant Misha adores working with him.

"Hi Carey! How are you today?" he asks as he stops to lean against the doorframe.

"I'm good, Michael. For a Monday, you know."

It's a lame attempt at humor, but he smiles, which is nice of him. "Speaking of it being Monday, I went up to see Randall, but his door is closed and the lights are off in his office. Is he out on a retrieval today?"

I shake my head and glance down at my calendar on my laptop screen before looking up at the assistant director of the museum. "Not that I have any record of. We have a pickup of a Rubik's cube that's supposedly one of the originals from the year they first released it this Friday, but I have nothing scheduled for today."

Michael draws his dark eyebrows in toward his nose and frowns. "Well, this is a mystery then because he's not here, and it's nearly ten o'clock. I don't think he's ever been this late."

"I know. It's very unlike him. Did you get to talk to him at the benefit Friday night? Maybe he mentioned something to you then?" I ask, quickly running through my conversations with Mr. James that night and coming up with nothing but his ominous warning about Nicholas.

Now it's Michael's turn to shake his head. "We didn't get to chat much that night. My wife arrived late, so I was on my own, so to speak, for the first hour of the party. I spent most of my time that night attempting to pry money out of donors' hands."

I can't help but find it odd that he insisted on mentioning his wife like that, but I've heard rumors around the office that more than a few of the people who work here would love to get to know Michael more, so maybe that's why he brought her up. He never used to until recently, and now this is the second time in as many conversations with me that he's done it.

A flash of worry spikes inside me for a moment at the idea that he thinks I'm one of those people who want to get to know him better. Is that why he's suddenly bringing up his wife whenever we talk?

"Well, I'm sure he'll be in today. I don't think Mr. James has ever missed a day of work. Even when he's on vacation, he always calls or videoconferences with me."

As much as I wish that wasn't true, it is. The man never truly leaves work in this building.

Michael's eyes get wide, and he throws his head back in laughter. "Maybe he's run off to start a new life. Wouldn't that be a trip?"

I laugh at the very thought of Randall James running off anywhere but especially to begin a new life. His life is this museum. I can't even imagine what he'd do if he wasn't the director here.

Probably shrivel up and die.

Then again, for the first time ever, he didn't call or text me over the weekend with some stupid questions that could have waited for work today, so maybe he did run off to somewhere. It takes me about two seconds to dismiss that idea as utterly ludicrous.

"You might be right. Maybe he'll call today from some beach in the Caribbean to tell me he's never coming back because suddenly he's decided to be a toes-in-the-sand guy who drinks umbrella drinks all day," I say with a smile, fine with joking about my boss's whereabouts since he's going to show up sometime today anyway.

Again, Michael laughs out loud because the thought is absurd. Mr. James would never abandon his job to become a beach bum or some island gigolo. It's just not his style.

To be honest, I can't imagine my boss ever going to a beach. All that sand would likely drive him out of his mind. He's far too fastidious to allow it to get into everything like it has a habit of doing whenever I go to the beach.

As he turns to leave, he says, "Thanks for that visual. I'm going to be chuckling to myself all day. If you hear from Randall, please tell him I need to speak to him."

"I will."

Alone with the image of Mr. James trying to seduce some woman on a beach somewhere filling my brain, I close my eyes and shake my head to get rid of that ridiculous thought. I have no idea where my boss is, but living in the tropics is one place I can safely bet he's not.

. . .

THE WEATHER IS perfect for lunch outside today since it's sunny without a cloud in the sky and nearly seventy degrees. At noon, Emory and I head outside to a picnic table on the side of the museum. We set up our bowls of salad from that place downtown we both love and dig in, loving how green everything around us is.

As she pours more olive oil on top of her cobb salad, she smiles. "This is the life."

I wish I could agree with her, but I don't get to set my own work schedule or take breaks whenever I want to, so this may be the life for her. For me, my day-to-day is just something I have to endure until I can find a better job. Since that's highly unlikely in the museum business considering my lack of an advanced degree, I better get used to this life, I guess.

"It is beautiful out here," I say as I eat a forkful of grilled chicken and a section of tomato with just the right amount of honey mustard salad dressing.

"So did bossman ever show up?" she asks with a laugh. Emory knows all too well how much my boss can irritate me sometimes.

I shake my head and shrug. "No, and it's very odd. Not that I'm sad about having a day off from him, especially after he pulled that weird, cryptic thing on me."

Emory sets her fork down in her plastic bowl and narrows her eyes. "You didn't tell me about whatever this thing is he did. What happened?"

After I finish another forkful of salad, I explain, "He saw me talking to his friend that night of the benefit, and I think he warned me about spending time with him. At least that's what it sounded like to my ears. It was very weird. Mr. James never gets involved in my personal life. It came out of left field."

A slow smile lifts the corners of her mouth. "Maybe he was jealous. I've always had a feeling your boss liked you more than just as a great assistant."

I can't stop my eyes from rolling into the back of my head at that idea. "God help me. No. Mr. Randall James does not like me that way. In fact, I'm not sure my boss likes any human beings, male or female, that way. If you aren't a toy, he has no interest in you."

With a devilish sparkle in her eyes, she chuckles. "Maybe he just needs to be introduced to another kind of toy, Carey. You never know. It might bring out the freak in him."

Suddenly, I feel like I'm going to be sick. Pushing my lunch away, I shake my head at the mere thought of anything sexual with my boss.

"Okay, now I'm done eating. Are you trying to make me throw up with talk like that?"

"He is a man, so unless he's dead from the waist down, it's entirely possible. I get emails from that company where I bought that warming lube that guy Jack used to like. Maybe your boss would be interested in looking at some of their other items. Not that the warming lube is bad, but maybe good old Mr. James would want to start in the beginners' section and work his way up to the good stuff."

I can't keep the grimace off my face as she discusses my boss like he's any normal man. "Can we talk about something else? I've already lost my appetite. I don't want to lose my lunch too."

She waves me off and moves her nearly finished salad off to the side. "Fine. Let's talk about that guy you met at the benefit Friday night. You said you hoped you two were going to go out Saturday night. How did that go?"

If it had happened at all, I would have told her about it already. Emory knows that, so this is her way of coaxing me into talking about why we didn't get together.

"He called me Saturday afternoon and had to beg off. He said he was going to call tonight, so we'll see."

"Are you going to answer the phone, or has he already failed the potential boyfriend test?" she asks, teasing me about my strict rules for men.

"Yes, I'm going to answer when he calls. I like him. He's good looking, and we had fun talking Friday night. I'm not crazy about him being friends with my boss, but it's not a deal breaker."

Emory's eyebrows shoot up into her forehead. "I'm surprised him bailing on your date wasn't a deal breaker. I do believe, Miss Mitchell, that you're willing to give men a chance again."

That gets her an eye roll. "I'm just saying I'll answer the phone. We aren't running off and getting married in Vegas. It's just a call. That's it."

I don't want to let on how much I hope Nicholas and I can get together and see if there's any chemistry between us. Emory has a habit of wanting to know every last detail when it comes to the men I date, and for this one, I'd like to play my cards close to the vest.

At least for a little while.

Sensing I won't be able to play coy if we stay out here at this picnic table much longer, I check my phone and say, "I better get back inside. My boss might be in the office by now, and God help me if he needs something and I'm not there. He's likely to have a meltdown."

I stand up to leave, and Emory follows me, grabbing the trash from our lunch. "Has anyone ever told him he's a diva?"

She throws everything into the nearby garbage can as I answer, "Yes, I'll be sure to say exactly that to him the day I win the lottery."

"I'm just saying the man is a handful, Carey, and I think you bear the brunt of it."

We walk back toward the front of the building as I silently agree with her. It's no use talking about this subject because she'll only tell me to leave and find another job. That's the free spirit artist in her. She doesn't understand the concept of staying just because I need to pay bills. That's entirely too pedestrian for her.

Halfway back, she grabs my arm to stop me. "Hey, what's going on in that upstairs window?"

I look up at where she's pointing and see what looks like a hand pressed against the glass through the blinds. "I don't know. That's the storage area on the third floor. Nobody goes up there."

Giggling, she elbows me in the arm. "Well, somebody has. I think it might be two somebodies, in fact."

Confused, I look at her for a long moment, and then I grasp her meaning. "Is sex the only thing on your mind today?"

"It's a normal thing to think about. We need to see what's going on up there," she says as she begins to pull me toward the front door.

"Can I tell you how much I don't want to catch two of my coworkers up there having a good time?"

"Ridiculous! Let's go see!"

I let myself get dragged into the building, all the while thinking I'm honestly dreading what I'll find upstairs. Who cares if two consenting adults want to have a little fun in one of the storage rooms? It's not anything I'd do, especially since I think that room they're in is the doll room and that place gives me the creeps every time I have to go up there, but who am I to say if they should have chosen a better place for a lunchtime quickie?

By the time we reach the third floor, I'm convinced I don't want to see whatever it is in that window, but Emory won't let me back out now. The storage area on this floor is filled mostly with toys that are what my boss calls one-offs, items that might be able to be displayed at some point if we can find others in that style but are no use until then, and dolls that need to be repaired. I try to avoid this area because dolls missing limbs or eyes or even their heads are unsettling on the best days and never fail to unnerve me every time I have to be around them.

"Ten to one it's a married guy doing his secretary," Emory whispers as we slowly walk toward the room.

I turn to look at her and shake my head. "You do realize no one calls them secretaries anymore."

"Sorry. A married guy doing his executive assistant. Same thing."

With every step, I feel more uneasy doing this. "When I have nightmares because of the dolls in that room, you're going to be okay with me calling you in the middle of the night, right?"

As we walk, she looks around at all the one-offs and shrugs. "I thought you didn't have nightmares. Anyway, if you do, I keep odd hours, so yeah, feel free to call me. Hey, what is that thing called a Pet Rock?"

I glance over at the brown cardboard box with those exact words printed on it in black and answer, "Just what it says. A rock people can keep as a pet."

"Seriously?"

Nodding, I smile at how silly it seems now. It must have seemed silly back when they were popular too, but people still bought them by the millions I think, strangely enough.

"Yeah. The seventies were wild."

"Definitely, but not in that way. Wild isn't exactly how I'd describe something so stupid, but okay. Are we almost to the room? They're probably back at their desks and dreaming about their next rendezvous by now," she complains.

I point at the door for the room and mouth, "Right here."

We both stand like we're frozen to the floor for a long moment before she whispers, "Well, open it. Time for cheaters to pay the piper."

"Why do you think they're suddenly cheaters?"

"Because only cheaters do it at work. People in a regular relationship just go to one of their houses. Now let's see who's behind door number one."

She's having far too good a time with this, but that's Emory for you. I'm more uncomfortable interrupting two people enjoying themselves, regardless of whether or not they're cheating.

I turn the doorknob and slowly open the door, hoping I'm giving the people inside enough time to at least cover up. Fully expecting to hear a scream, I'm surprised when I'm met with silence.

"No cheaters or anyone else up here," I say, pushing the door all the way open. "Your eyes must have been playing tricks on you."

Before she can answer, I flip on the light switch next to the door, and then I scream louder than I've ever before in my life. It's not the weirdly disfigured dolls that frighten me.

It's Mr. James still dressed in his tux he wore to the benefit Friday night with a rope around his neck hanging from the ceiling.

Dead.

9

For hours, the police question everyone in the building about when they saw Mr. James last, what his usual routine regarding each of us was, and our whereabouts since Friday. Surprise immediately tore through the museum at the news that our director had been found hanged to death in an upstairs storage room, but no one was more shocked than Emory and I since we found him.

The policemen separate us, probably hoping to find out if either one of us is lying about anything, and for nearly an hour, an officer named Thompson questions me about everything from how long I've worked at the museum to what the last thing Mr. James said to me when I saw him at the benefit.

"Whatever you can tell us will be helpful. I'm told by a Mr. Michael Tanner that you were closest to Mr. James out of everyone here. He mentioned you and Mr. James worked closely together to organize the fundraising event last week. I just need you to try to remember everything your boss said to you that night."

Unsure his exact last words are necessary and not wanting to share my private life with the officer, I explain Friday night was very busy for us, so I didn't get to speak to him much at the event.

"You have to understand that Mr. James's focus was on the donors who would contribute to keep the museum going. I'm not sure if you know much about museums, Officer Thompson, but raising money is one of the primary jobs for someone in his position. While there are grants museums can apply for, much of our funding is from individuals and corporations who choose to donate to keep the doors open."

The officer nods, and I notice his shirt collar is so tight that whenever he lowers his head, he instantly grows a double chin. He's not a fat man, so the effect is striking. It makes me want to reach over and undo that top button so he can breathe a little easier.

"I understand, ma'am. So you're saying the victim spent most of his time Friday night talking to guests?"

The victim. Just hearing those words makes my stomach turn. Not Mr. James. Not Randall or Randall James. The victim.

"Yes. We spoke very little."

That's technically a lie, but I like to think it's more like a tiny fib than a full-fledged untruth. Nothing Mr. James said to me about Nicholas would be useful to the investigation of his death anyway.

He hanged himself. Suicide doesn't include any guilty parties.

After another twenty minutes of Officer Thompson grilling me about everything from the time Mr. James may have left the building that night to what he usually did on the weekends, finally, he closes his notebook and nods his head. I silently thank God the interrogation is over and I can finally have some time to myself to grieve my boss's death.

"If we have any other questions, we'll be in touch, Miss Mitchell."

Curious what else he'd need to know, I look up at him when he stands to leave and say, "I'm confused. Mr. James killed himself, didn't he? I'm not sure why all this investigation into a suicide is happening."

Even as I say that, I have a hard time reconciling how much he loved this museum with the horrible thought that he arranged to take his life in the very building that meant so much to him. It doesn't make sense.

The officer doesn't answer for a long moment before finally saying, "Miss Mitchell, Mr. James did not hang himself. He was murdered. We'll be in touch if we have any more questions."

I feel my mouth drop open at his stunning statement. Murdered? No, that's not possible. I saw him hanging from the ceiling. Hanging means suicide, doesn't it?

Officer Thompson leaves me sitting alone in utter shock. Who would want to murder Mr. James?

Yes, he was difficult to work for sometimes, but certainly not bad enough to wish dead. The man loved toys, for God's sake. He believed in this museum with all his heart. He devoted his life to this place to the exclusion of having any real personal life outside of the museum. He didn't even have an ex-wife or husband with an axe to grind.

Who would want to kill someone like that?

As all of these questions swirl around in my mind, Nicholas walks into my office, surprising me. "What are you doing here?"

Instantly, I realize that sounds terrible, so I quickly add, "I mean, we just found out Mr. James is dead."

Then it dawns on me Nicholas isn't just a man I'm interested in. He was a friend of my boss.

"I'm so sorry for your loss. I'm just a little frazzled right now. That's why I don't seem to know my manners. Please, sit down."

Nicholas takes a seat in the only chair in front of my desk and reaches out to touch my hand. "I'm sure you're more than a little frazzled, Carey. I came over as soon as I heard what happened. Is it true you found him?"

I nod, unable to answer the single word yes without crying. I found him. Dead. Hanging from the ceiling with a rope tied around his neck. His face blue, his dark eyes lifeless. Still wearing his tux from the benefit three days ago.

"It's okay. You don't need to talk about it. I'm sure you've talked about it enough for a lifetime today. How about I drive you home so you can make a nice pot of tea and curl up to watch your favorite show?"

I know he's trying to be nice, but sitting alone in my apartment watching TV is the last thing on my mind. In fact, being alone isn't on my list of things I want anytime soon.

"Thank you, but I need to stick around for my friend. She was with me when I found him."

Nicholas gives me a kind smile that helps more than he can ever understand. "Okay. I'll call you later."

"Thanks. I just don't want to leave her alone after seeing that."

As he stands to leave, he says, "You're a good friend, Carey. There's no need to explain. I'll give you a call in a few hours and see if you need anything."

He takes a few steps before I realize I haven't said much about him losing a friend in such a horrible way. "Nicholas, wait."

Looking back, he seems confused, so I hurry over to where he's standing near my office door. "I've been so consumed with myself. I'm sorry. Your friend is gone. How are you feeling? Are you okay? How was it for you talking to the police? They say he was murdered. I thought it was suicide because of how I found him, but that officer who talked with me said someone murdered him. I can't believe it."

Nicholas nods and sighs heavily. "I think I might be in shock. Randall was the director of a toy museum. Who on earth would want to hurt someone like that? I mean, I know he could be a bear when it came to working for him. You know that's true. That doesn't translate into someone wanting to kill him. I just don't understand how this happened. I told the police as much as I could remember from Friday's event, but nothing seemed to point to someone murdering him."

My boss's words about this man echo in my head, and I can't imagine what Mr. James was talking about. Nicholas Madera has been nothing but charming and kind. What could he have been referring to when he told me to be careful?

"I'll be around all night, so please call. We can talk about it, or we can talk about anything else. Whatever we need to, okay?"

With a smile, he leans down and presses a soft kiss to my cheek. "You're a sweet person, Carey. Thank you. I hope your friend is going to be okay."

"Thanks. I'll talk to you later."

I follow him out into the hallway to find Emory waiting outside. She watches him walk past and gives me one of her "he's fine" looks when I stop in front of her.

"So that's the guy? I approve, Carey. He knows how to wear a suit. That's for sure," she says a little too loudly.

"Shhh. I don't want him to hear that. We're in mourning, remember?"

My friend sighs before standing up. "I didn't know the man, Carey. I mean, I'm not insensitive, so I'm here for you, but he wasn't anyone to me. I'm sorry for what happened to him, but I'm more concerned about you. How are you holding up? Those cops grilled me to within an inch of my life. I can only imagine what they did with you since you were the guy's assistant."

We walk back to my office as I explain what Officer Thompson told me about Mr. James being murdered. Emory seems as shocked as I was.

"What? He was hanging. Isn't that suicide?" she asks as she plops down into the chair in front of my desk.

I shrug, unsure what to say. "I don't know. I naturally thought he killed himself. Who's ever heard of someone killing a person by hanging? On top of that, who would want to kill Mr. James?"

Emory gives me a tiny smile. "Haven't you ever heard of people wanting to off their bosses? There's a whole show on that very topic on the Discovery Channel, I think. Or maybe that murder channel. What is that called? I can't remember."

If she's suggesting anyone here is responsible for my boss's death, she's crazy. Everyone who works for the museum may think he was a pain in the ass every so often but not enough to wish him dead. That's crazy.

"Nobody here did it. I'd bet money on that. Mr. James might have been a taskmaster from time to time, but I simply can't believe any of my coworkers did this. No way."

"I'm just saying people have been known to lose it on their boss. The only person here I can absolutely say I know for sure didn't do it is you. You couldn't hurt a fly, much less kill a man by lifting him up and hanging him from the ceiling."

Even though I know my friend is trying to help, I still can't help but cringe at her explanation of how I'm not capable of killing Randall James. "Don't talk like that. I can't think of his death in that way. Not yet."

"Okay. I'm just saying even though he was a Jack Sprat kind of guy and even if you wanted to hang him from a rope tied to the ceiling, you couldn't."

Before I can tell her to not say that again, the assistant director of the museum pokes his head into my office. "Carey, I'm going to talk to everyone in my office before dismissing all the staff. I'm heading down right now."

"Okay, Michael. I'll be right there."

I tidy up the papers on my desk for a moment or two before saying to Emory, "I'll be back. I can't imagine what he's going to say. What does a person say when a murder occurs at their workplace? God, I can't believe this happened."

My friend pats my hand and smiles sweetly. "I'll be here. Take your time, honey. We'll go back to your apartment and take it easy when you're done."

She has no idea how thankful I am she's going to be with me for the rest of the day. I thought I'd need to be there for her, but the truth is I'm barely keeping things together. My emotions are all over the place, and controlling them is becoming harder and harder as the minutes go by and everything becomes more real.

My boss is dead. Someone murdered him. What's going to happen to the museum now? All of these questions march through my mind over and over, but I have no answers.

When I get to Michael's office, everyone else on staff is already there. They all wear expressions of shock and disbelief I know are exactly like the one I've had on my face since I first saw Mr. James upstairs in that storage room.

Misha Monroe, the older woman who holds the same job I do but for the assistant director, hurries over to me when I stop just inside the door. A kind person, she always smells like the perfume my mother used to wear, so every time I'm around her, it's naturally comforting.

"Oh, sweetie. I've been wanting to see you since I found out. I heard you found him. How are you holding up? I can't imagine seeing that," she says in a voice tinged with tears.

When she takes my hands in hers, I almost lose control. I've been on the verge of crying for hours, but now I can barely compose myself in front of her.

I hang my head and quietly say, "I'm a mess, Misha. After Michael talks to us, I'm going to go home and cry. I don't want to do it here at work, but I'm having a hard time keeping things together."

She leans forward and hugs me like she usually does when we talk, and that's all it takes. The waterworks start, and I can't stop them. I'm not someone who likes to show her emotions at work, but I'm unable to keep them inside anymore.

"Let it out, honey. You're always so strong, but you're a human being, and this has been such a hard day. I know you'll miss him. He was a son of a bitch sometimes, but he was our leader. We loved him, even if he drove us crazy."

Her words and embrace make me feel so much better, so by the time Michael walks into his office, I'm able to face what he has to tell us all. I look over at where he stands near his desk and see he's having a hard time too.

"Okay, everyone. I won't keep us here much longer because I know we all need to go home and put this day behind us. Randall James will be missed. He was the one soul who made this museum what it was. He loved toys and believed they deserved a place to be showcased. His leadership has helped us become a destination for kids of all ages to learn and enjoy the idea of play."

Michael stops when he gets choked up and has to take a moment to compose himself. Taking a deep breath, he lets it out slowly, like this entire day has been too much for him.

"The museum will be closed indefinitely until the police are finished with their investigation. I wish I could say it will be a paid vacation, but the museum simply doesn't have the budget for that. If you have vacation or sick days, you may take them so you'll get paid for at least some time off. I hope we will all be back within a week or so, but I can make no promises at this time. I'll be the acting director for the time being, so any questions you may have, you can ask me. For today, I want you to go home and relax. I'll be in touch with everyone once I know more."

The twelve people in the room with us talk in hushed tones as they file out of his office. Michael waves me over to him, so I thank Misha and head over to his desk.

"Carey, I'm so sorry for what you've been through today. Finding him must have been so terrible. I wish I could help more than just saying kind words."

I smile at how considerate he is. "I'm okay, Michael. I just want to go home and try to forget."

"Trust me, I understand," he says, nodding. "You'll continue to be the assistant to the museum's director, but until a new one is hired, you'll be reporting to me. That's when we all get back here, which I hope will be within the week. When that happens is up to the police, though."

Assuming the police have informed him of the reality of what happened to Mr. James, I lower my voice and say, "I can't believe anyone would kill him. Who could do that? Yes, he could be intense when it came to his work, but why would anyone murder him?"

Michael shakes his head. "I have no idea. I've been thinking the very same thing. Randall was a piece of work on occasion. He certainly cared more about the museum than people's feelings sometimes, but I can't see anyone doing this to him. Not for being short on a phone call or dressing someone down for something they did that he didn't approve of. I can't see it, Carey."

"The police asked me if he had enemies, but I told him I didn't know him outside of work. I got the feeling they didn't think it was anyone here, but if that's the case, then someone came here on Friday night to kill him. How could that be?"

"I'm at a loss with this. I just can't believe this happened. Can you post about us closing on whatever social media the museum is on? I'd appreciate it. Misha said she's going to hang a sign on the front doors, so anyone who doesn't know what happened and comes here next week will see that."

"Sure, Michael. I'll take care of it."

He looks relieved as he nods his head, but I have a feeling his mind is far away from this office at the moment. "I've got a million things to deal with, so go home and take care of yourself. I'll be in touch when I know when we're opening up again."

I thank him and go back to my office to find Emory. As much as I want to just go home and crawl into bed to hide under the covers, I need to handle the social media posts first.

She stands as I walk in, but I shake my head. "I have one thing to do, and then we can go."

After I take my seat at my desk, she sits back down. "Are they actually making you do work? Now? Seems a little ridiculous to me. For God's sake, you just found a guy dead, Carey."

I search through my graphics to find the one I posted when the museum's plumbing went haywire and flooded the bathrooms on the first floor, forcing us to close for a week last year, and explain to her what I need to do. "Not work. Michael just asked me to post on social media. It is part of my job, after all."

That's enough to shame her into silence for a few moments. I quickly whip up a new graphic that states the museum will be closed until further notice and we hope to open back up as soon as possible. After posting it to the various social media platforms I always post to, I close my laptop and take a deep breath in, wishing it would clear away how awful I feel.

It doesn't work.

"Ready?"

Emory stands up again and smiles. "Yeah. Let's get you out of here."

I turn off my office light and close the door behind me. After the day I've had, all I want to do is be in my own house, safe and sound.

10

Emory hands me a glass of her favorite drink, and even though I'm not a fan of margaritas, I can use something to take the edge off this day. "Drink this. I made a pitcher for us, but I can make more too. Today feels like a day to drink until you forget."

I take a sip and wish I liked tequila more. "I'm not much of a drinker, you know."

Laughing, she sits down on the other end of the sofa from me and takes a big gulp of her drink. "Nobody says you have to be. Just enjoy it and take things easy. You've had a hell of a day, Carey."

"I didn't even realize I had any liquor here," I say, wondering when I would have bought a bottle of tequila. Then I remember that party last summer. "Oh, it must have been when we all got together last July."

My friend laughs at me. "You know, if you have to try to remember the last time you had a party, it's time for another one."

"It feels wrong talking about a party right now, Emory," I scold her.

Clearly, she's not having a hard time with what happened. I guess that's not surprising. Emory has never been one of those tender souls who falls apart when things get bad. She's much tougher than I am.

"My bad," she says with her best attempt at looking sorry. "I was just trying to get your mind off the current situation."

I take another sip of my drink and set the margarita glass on the coffee table in front of me. Leaning back, I curl up under my favorite black and white checked throw with Scottie dogs on it and bring my knees up to my chest. All I want to do is rest here and try to forget everything that's happened today.

After a few minutes of us sitting in silence, I say, "You know, I just can't wrap my head around it. Someone killed my boss. I don't know what to think. Was I in danger? Is it wrong to ask that? I don't want to sound selfish or self-involved, but he was closest to me at the museum."

Emory pats my arm sympathetically, but she doesn't have the answers either. "I honestly can't say why someone did that to him, but I doubt you were in danger, Carey. I'm not thinking this murder had anything to do with the museum or what you guys do there. I'm guessing, and I could be completely off the mark here, but I'm going to say what happened to him had to do with his personal life."

God, I want to believe that, but if that's the case, why kill him at the museum?

"Then why did they do it where they did? Mr. James had a house. Granted, he was a workaholic, so he spent a lot of his time at work, but he went home every night. Why wouldn't someone go after him there?"

She thinks about that for a few seconds and answers, "Maybe they didn't know where he lived, but they knew where he worked. To be honest, Carey, I'm thinking the police must be looking at the guest list for the benefit last week because that's probably when it happened."

That little nugget of truth settles into my brain, and I can't help but think I was the last person who may have seen him alive. "Emory, I talked to Mr. James after the benefit ended. I saw him in one of the collections rooms. He came to find me."

"Really? Why? I bet it was to tell you he needed you to do something for him, wasn't it?"

I shake my head as the memory of my conversation with him—our last conversation—replays in my mind. "No. He wanted to warn me about something."

Emory looks intrigued as she raises her eyebrows to show her surprise. "Warn you about something? Do tell."

I sigh, hating what I have to say now. "I don't know why he said this, but he warned me to be careful with Nicholas. I didn't understand why, though. He and Nicholas are friends." I stop for a moment and correct myself. "Were friends."

Tears well in my eyes as I say that. I just can't get my mind to accept Mr. James is gone.

But Emory is curious about his warning and asks, "Do you think he knew something he wanted to tell you later but didn't get a chance to? Maybe there's something about Nicholas you should be concerned about."

"Like what? You saw him. He's a perfectly normal guy."

My friend levels her gaze on my face like she can't believe I'm this naïve. "Perfectly normal guys have pasts, you know. Maybe your boss wanted to give you a head's up about his. I don't know why he couldn't just tell you right then and there, though. Was your boss usually a mysterious guy?"

I think about that question for a few seconds. Mr. James a mysterious man? Not really. Then again, I didn't know him personally. All our interactions involved work. That's it. What he did in his private life he kept completely to himself.

"No, I wouldn't describe him as mysterious. Intense, in that he was one hundred percent about work when he was in the building, but no, I can't see anyone thinking Mr. James was mysterious."

She takes a gulp of her drink. "The guy had to have a private life. That you knew nothing of it and you were his assistant tells me he had to be at least a little mysterious."

"He was private. There's a difference."

Emory nods and then tilts her head left and right like she's weighing my comment for its validity. "Fair enough, but he must have had things going on in his private life. Was he straight? Did he have a girlfriend? Or was he gay and had a boyfriend?"

I stare at her as I try to remember a single time my boss even vaguely referenced any romantic entanglement. I honestly have no idea if he was straight or gay or if he was involved with anyone. All I knew about Mr. James was he cared deeply about the toy museum and came to work every day, Monday through Friday. He wore a dark suit every day I worked with him, only changing his dress shirt each day. Not that he ever got very adventurous with those. He mostly wore white and gray shirts with the occasional pink or blue shirt popping up in his wardrobe.

God, I know nothing about a man I worked with for three years. How can that be? We must have had at least one conversation about our lives outside of work.

Didn't we?

Over and over, I go through every time we talked while I worked with him, and nothing personal comes up. Is it possible I've simply forgotten those comments? He had to have mentioned what he did on a long weekend or some wedding he had to attend. Everyone drops those little details into work conversations.

Finally, I have to admit the truth. The man I worked with for years was a complete stranger to me.

"I have no idea, Emory. He may have been a monk for all I know," I say, sad to confess someone so integral to my life was someone I knew so little about.

For some reason, that makes her eyes grow wide. "Now there's a mystery for you. Man who worked as the director of a toy museum was secretly a monk and some vicious killer targeted him for murder, but why? That's the key."

I roll my eyes at her fabricated nonsense. "I didn't mean literally. And that sounds like something you'd watch on Lifetime, like that movie the other night about the woman whose doctor impregnated her and then turned out to be an assassin. Ridiculous."

"Well, I was just trying to help. You know, to cheer you up a little."

I hang my head and let out a heavy sigh. "I know. Thanks for that. I think I just want to go to bed."

"Are you sure? It's not even four o'clock in the afternoon."

Throwing off my blanket, I stand up and grab my drink. "I know, but I'm exhausted. Thanks for coming over to hang out with me. I think I was worried about you after finding him with me, but the truth is I'm the mess and you're doing fine. I wish I was."

Emory follows me to the kitchen with her glass and finishes her drink as I throw mine down the drain. "I can stay while you sleep if you don't want to be alone."

"No, I'm fine. Thanks, though. I appreciate the offer."

She opens her arms and gives me a bear hug before starting for the door. "I'm going home and hope the muses have something for me. Call me if you need anything, okay? I mean that."

I nod and give her a smile. "Thanks. I'll call you. Right now, I'm going to crawl into bed and pull the covers over my head. Maybe if I do that the memory of today will disappear."

My friend who rarely bothers with the sentimental like I do shakes her head. "It won't, but you'll be okay. I'll grab Jenna sometime this week, and we can all go out for a bite to eat. Does that sound okay?"

"Yeah. Thanks again, Emory."

She waves goodbye and walks out, leaving me alone

in my apartment wishing I had a roommate. It's not that I didn't love having her here this afternoon, but Emory and her tough skin about things isn't what I need today.

What I actually need or want I'm unsure, but I'm a little too sensitive right now for her jokes.

And then on what may be the worst day of my life, my ex texts me and makes it so much worse. I ignore it, but he proceeds to send me five more messages right in a row in the next few minutes, and even though I know I shouldn't, I read them.

Each one says the same thing. He wants me back. He's never going to let me go. I need to come back to him.

I really can't deal with this, so I turn off my phone and set it on my nightstand before pulling the covers over my head. If he can't reach me, he can't upset me.

By Wednesday, I'm feeling much better so when Nicholas asks to come over to see me, I say yes and hope after nearly two days of crying that I don't look like someone's been pummeling my eyes nonstop. I like him, but I can't help but wonder if it's wrong or at least in poor taste to spend time together for any reason other than sympathizing with him.

I have little food in the house since I've been holed up in my apartment for two days, but I whip up a few snacks with the cheese I have in the refrigerator and crackers that aren't too stale yet. One look in the mirror after I put my makeup on says I've been a mess since he last saw me. There's nothing I can do about that, though. Sadness isn't easily hidden on my face, unfortunately.

When I answer the door, he's standing in front of me dressed in a pair of jeans and a light blue T-shirt. I don't know why I assumed he'd look the same as the few times I've seen him in a suit and tie, but I can't hide my surprise when I see him.

He picks up on it immediately and smiles when he sees my eyes open wide in astonishment. "I hope that look isn't because I look bad. I figured since I'm off the clock, I should be comfortable."

I step back and let him into my apartment, thankful I didn't choose that navy blue dress I was considering. "You look great. I think I was just expecting you to look like you always do, which is crazy since we've only talked twice."

Looking around as I walk by into the kitchen, he says, "You have a nice place here. Very cozy."

My boss's warning to me to be careful repeats in my head, and I can't help but wonder if Nicholas means tiny and poor when he says cozy. Why did Mr. James say that to me? I hate that it's tainting my time with this man.

I decide to push my boss's words out of my mind and offer Nicholas a seat in my living room filled with cheap furniture. "Please, sit down. I didn't have much in the house, but I made some little snacks for us."

As I set the tray with the cheese and crackers down on the coffee table, he says, "You didn't have to do that, but thank you. I just wanted to see you and make sure you're okay. It's not every day someone goes through what you went through."

My heart sinks at hearing him say that. Is he only here because I found a man hanging from the ceiling? Should I think he's not interested in me anymore?

"Oh. I'm okay," I say as I sit down next to him. "I guess you can tell I've been crying since my eyes are all puffy. How have you been doing? I feel like you're suffering more than anyone at work because you knew him personally. I just knew him as the man I reported to at the museum."

I hate how dismissive that sounds, but these last few days of racking my brain to think of who may have wanted to kill Mr. James has shown I didn't know him at all. I have to think Nicholas knew him far better.

When he answers, though, I get the sense he didn't really know the man at all either. "To be honest, Randall and I called each other friends, but I mainly knew him because I donated to the museum one time a few years ago. Ever since, we've been on speaking terms and I always get an invite to any event happening there."

I don't know why his not knowing my boss well is dismaying, but it is. I guess I had hoped to glean something from Nicholas tonight about who the man I worked for was and who harbored such ugly feelings about him. Now it seems I won't get those answers.

"So you weren't close?" I ask, confused even more about my boss's warning about being careful with Nicholas.

If Mr. James only knew the man socially, what made him find me Friday night to caution me about him?

Nicholas shakes his head and shrugs. "Not really. We talked at events we both attended. You'd be surprised at how many there are in this area. It's a small group of people with money around here, so it's like a circuit. We all travel from event to event donating to causes we care about."

The way he mentions Mr. James like he had money to give surprises me. I never thought of him as wealthy. I know he wasn't getting paid that much to be director of the museum.

"I don't want this to sound rude, but are you saying Mr. James was at those events as a donor?"

Nodding, Nicholas leans forward to grab a cracker with a slice of cheese on top of it. "Yes."

Still needing a little more than just that one word answer, I wait as he eats his snack and when he finishes, I say, "Again, please don't think I'm trying to be indelicate about the man, but I didn't think he had any money to donate to anything. Museum director at a museum like ours is not a notoriously well-paying job."

Nicholas chuckles. "Oh, that's not where he got his money. His wife is where the money comes from. Not Randall, for sure."

A wife? Oh my God! My boss was married, and I never knew. So much for my friends always claiming he had a thing for me.

I sit back on the sofa in utter shock. "I had no idea there was a Mrs. James. He didn't wear a wedding band, so I think I just assumed he wasn't married. God, I feel so foolish now. I had no idea my boss, the man I worked with, was married."

With a smile, Nicholas says, "Was married is the correct way to say it. Elise died a year ago after them being married for nearly a decade. He seemed to take it very hard, if the stories I heard are true. It was Elise James who was the one who loved charities, not Randall. To be honest, I don't think he cared about any of them he gave to, other than the museum. That place was his pride and joy, especially after she passed."

I know my mouth is hanging open as I listen to him describe a man and his life I knew nothing of. "He had a wife who died a year ago? He never said a thing. I never knew he was mourning anyone last year. Oh, God. I feel like he was a total stranger to me now. No wonder that officer looked at me so strangely when I couldn't answer a single question about what he did outside of work. You'd think I'd know something about this."

Nicholas softly pats my knee to comfort me. "I wouldn't beat myself up over it. To be honest, I don't think the people who work with me know much about what I do outside of work. It's not like you and Randall got together to drink beers at the local pub after hours."

Blowing the air out of my mouth, I shake my head. "I had no idea he even drank beer. God, how is it possible you can work with someone for years and not know these important things about them?"

With a smile, he says, "I don't think it's important that you didn't know he drank beer, although I don't think he did."

I nudge him, knowing he's trying to lighten the mood. "Not that, silly. I just think the person who worked so closely with him at the museum should know he was married and then became a widower."

And to think I entertained the possibility that Mr.

James was gay when Emory asked me about him the other day.

Nicholas pats my leg again but doesn't move his hand when he stops, leaving it to rest on my knee. "Don't beat yourself up about this, Carey. Randall kept his life very private. You're not to blame for that. He is."

I want to defend my boss, but I don't know what to say. Like Emory, Nicholas doesn't seem torn up about Mr. James's passing, as awful as it was.

It seems I'm the only one who's bothered. God, that's sad.

11

For two nights in a row, Nicholas and I hang out in my apartment getting to know one another, and I have to admit he makes me feel better. My ex texting me on a daily basis with messages that are becoming increasingly unhinged has the opposite effect, but I keep reminding myself that whatever he and I had is over.

I consider telling Nicholas about him because I spend each night we're together worrying the entire time that Chase is going to knock on my door and cause a scene, although it seems very early in our relationship to bring in any discussion of exes. No better way to kill the vibe than the introduction of the "I have a crazy ex-boyfriend" topic into any conversation.

Even though he doesn't seem torn up by the death of his friend, I'm still dealing with it in the best way possible. I think the way Nicholas is handling his loss is admirable, and I wish I could be more like him. He's stoic about the whole thing, while I'm constantly on the verge of tears.

Some part of me feels like a hypocrite after all the times I complained about my boss over the years, like something in my brain keeps whispering, "Nobody is buying this sad girl routine, Carey. They know what you thought of him. These crocodile tears of yours are fooling no one."

It's not that I was close to him or cared deeply about him. In fact, he drove me crazy many days with his perfectionist tendencies and need to harp on mistakes repeatedly. Does that mean I shouldn't feel bad I saw him hanging from the ceiling in that storage room surrounded by all those broken dolls?

Nicholas keeps telling me I shouldn't beat myself up over this. He says people mourn in different ways, and being the person who found him, I'm expected to experience this more intensely than others.

I want to believe him, especially since Emory said basically the same thing to me yesterday. She's so much stronger than I am, though, so I'm not surprised she's handling all of this better than me.

All of this rolls around my brain as I lie here in bed staring up at the ceiling wondering if I should get up to start my day. A quick glance over at my phone tells me it's after nine already. I can't remember the last time I was still in bed at this time of day before this week.

I didn't sleep well last night. I can't be sure, but I think I had a nightmare. That's strange because I don't experience them. I never have. Even as a child, I didn't have nightmares. Once when I watched a horror movie I had a weird dream, but it wasn't what anyone would call terrifying.

This one was all about Mr. James. I saw him hanging there in that storage room, and he looked like he was talking to me, but I couldn't hear him. He looked so pale, like someone had drained all the blood out of his face, and his lips appeared very dry, almost as if all the saliva had been sucked out of his mouth. His upper lip in particular seemed parched and stuck to his teeth.

That's all I remember about the dream. Not terribly scary, I guess, but just the image I have in my head from that moment I opened the door and saw him there that won't go away.

My mother used to praise me for not scaring easily. To her, that was something admirable. I'm not sure why I don't frighten like other people. A former friend who I don't speak to anymore got angry at me one time when I told her I don't have nightmares because most things don't bother me. She said that the reason scary things don't bother me is I'm not smart enough to know I should be scared.

Maybe she was right. I don't know. All I know is even though I found Mr. James dead, what bothers me most is how sad I am. We weren't close, and I've found out in the past few days that I barely knew much about him at all, but his passing saddens me more than I guess I expected it would.

Determined to make this a good day, I roll out of bed and pad out to the kitchen to make myself a coffee. The smell of it in the bag actually wakes me up more than my actual drinking it, but it's become a habit to down a couple cups of coffee every morning.

As my morning drink brews, filling my apartment

with the rich scent of French roast, I walk over to the window in my living room to see what the day is like outside. Pulling open the dark blue curtains that have lived up to the blackout claim on the package, I see the sun's out and the parents of those teenage boys who spend their nights keeping the rest of my apartment complex awake until all hours are enjoying some quiet time on their patio. For a moment, I consider the idea of interrupting their peaceful morning like they let their kids do to the rest of us every night, but with a shrug, I let that vengeful thought pass.

I trudge back to the kitchen, but on my way I see something white on the floor near the front door. When I walk closer, I see it's an envelope.

Maybe Nicholas slipped a little note under my door. He's sweet, so I can see him doing something romantic like that.

Bending down, I grab it and head back to the kitchen to get my coffee that's nearly finished brewing. I pour myself a cup and stand at the counter to read my letter.

What a nice gesture! I can't imagine what Mr. James was warning me about. Nicholas has been nothing but a perfect gentleman, and now this seals the deal.

There's no name on the front of the envelope, so I rip open the flap and pull out a single sheet of white paper. With a single glance, my stomach drops.

It's not a love letter from Nicholas.

My eyes skim over the words as disbelief fills me. There's no name to tell me who it's from, but whoever wrote it starts the letter by saying they're upset I haven't answered their messages in Instagram. I shake my head in confusion. What messages?

I continue reading, my stomach twisting into a tight knot. They say they know how I felt about my boss and how I'm relieved he's dead. They say he got what he deserved, just like I will soon enough.

Then I read the last line and my heart skips a beat. *I'm always watching you, so don't think I don't know everything.*

I drop the letter onto the counter and back away in horror until I run into the wall. Staring at the white sheet of paper, I shake my head, unable to understand why anyone would send such a letter to me. I never wished for Mr. James to die. I'm utterly torn up about his passing.

Worse, what do they mean they're watching me and know everything? What is there to know? I'm just an unknown woman who works for a man who was murdered. I had nothing to do with that. Who would be so cruel to write me something like this?

I cover my mouth as bile begins to creep up into my throat. Feeling like I'm going to be sick, I run to the bathroom and barely get the lid up in time before I throw up into the toilet. Tears stream down my cheeks with each time my stomach pushes up its contents and I retch.

When I finally think there's nothing left inside me, I collapse onto the tile floor and sob. None of this makes sense. I've never done anything to deserve that letter. Who could have written it? And why? And what do they mean they're watching me?

My mind flashes to all the times in the past week when I felt like I wasn't alone. That time at work. That time after the drunk guy followed Emory and me from the restaurant. That time when I went down to the dumpster to throw out my garbage. Was I right that someone was nearby?

Who could be behind this? Immediately, I think of my ex. It's typical of what Chase would do. His texts haven't had the desired effect he was looking for, so he's decided to turn up the terror now that he found out what happened to my boss.

I won't let him do this to me. No way. I broke up with him, and nothing he can do will make me go back to him.

After I rinse out my mouth and brush my teeth, I hurry to my bedroom to get my phone. I shouldn't read the messages they claimed they sent on Instagram, but I can't stop myself. I check my personal account and find nothing. Did they send them to the museum account? I'd never check there for private messages.

A few taps on my phone later and the messages come up. I read them and shake my head in disbelief. Someone has been watching me? For how long? Why? Who could this be?

Why do they make it sound like I deserve to be scared?

It has to be my ex. It smacks so much of him, even though Chase has never been much of a writer.

I can't read any more, so I close Instagram and call Jenna. If I wanted to talk about anything else, I'd talk to Emory, but she's always hated Chase, even when he wasn't being a cheating bastard. I know her. She'll rant and rave about how she always knew he was a jackass and how I should have listened to her. Right now, I just can't deal with that.

Thankfully, Jenna is awake, even though it's early for her, and without saying hello, I launch into what's happened. "I'm sorry to be calling at this hour, but I need to talk to someone. I got a letter today threatening me, and I'm more than a little freaked out. Then I found out I've been getting threatening private messages on the museum's Instagram account, and I read them. They're horrible!"

"Whoa. Slow down, Carey. What are you talking about? What letter? What messages?" Jenna asks in a sleepy voice.

Pacing across my living room, I yank the curtains closed. I try to answer her questions, but my mind is racing. "I got a letter this morning saying I wanted my boss to die. Why would someone say that? And then at the end of the letter, they said they're always watching me. And the messages are all about how this person knows me and is watching me. I'm scared, Jenna."

She's silent for so long that I wonder if the call dropped, but then she says in a quiet voice, "Wow, okay. You never get scared like you sound now. I'm sorry about what happened. Emory told me you guys found your boss hanging at the museum. You must have been so freaked out about that."

"Thanks, but this has me really freaked out, to be honest. Someone says they're watching me, Jenna. The other stuff was bad enough, but watching me? What am I going to do?"

On my way past my front door, I check to make sure it's locked. God only knows if whoever wrote that letter is still nearby. They had to walk right up to my apartment to slip that letter under the door. God, they were just feet away from me as I slept.

"Okay, calm down. We'll figure this out. Any chance it's someone playing a prank on you?" she asks before adding, "You know, like that ex-boyfriend of yours."

I stop pacing in front of my big window in the living room to pull the curtain back only an inch to look out, unsure what I'm looking for. "I thought of that. Maybe. I don't know. He has been texting me wanting to get back together."

"You know I liked him when you two were together, but if it's him, I say to hell with that bastard. First he cheats on you, and then he pulls this high school bullshit? That's not cool."

"What am I going to do?" I ask as I scan the parking lot for anything suspicious, although I have no idea what that would look like.

"Maybe you should call the police," she suggests. "I don't know what they'll be able to do, but it sounds like something for them to know."

"Do they really have time for someone getting a threatening letter and a few ugly messages? I'm no celebrity, you know. Do the police really care when normal people have this happen?"

She thinks about it for a few moments and sighs. "Point taken. It's hard enough getting the cops to come when there's something big going on. We had to call them at the restaurant last week when some drunk guy and his friends came in and started getting ugly with the other guests, threatening them and spilling drinks on people, and I swear to you it took two hours before the cops finally showed up. I get it wasn't a robbery or someone setting the place on fire, but things got out of hand quickly, and the poor waitstaff had to deal with those assholes. But they have more than enough time to badger me when that ex of mine goes missing."

"So what should I do?" I ask again, feeling like between us we surely can come up with an answer.

"Okay, let me think. You believe it's Chase, right? Call him and tell him you know what's going on. Take away his power. That should set him straight and make you feel better," Jenna suggests.

It's not a bad plan, but I'm not sure about actually confronting my ex. He's not stable, by any means, and I don't know what my saying I know it's him behind all this will do. He'll likely just lie and say it wasn't him. Then I'll be nowhere better than I am right now but he'll have gotten to speak to me. I really don't want to give him that.

"I don't know. I'll think about it."

"Do you want me to come over? I don't have work until four today, and since I'm up, I can grab a shower and be there in an hour."

As much as I know Jenna's trying to help, I don't feel much like socializing right now. My emotions are sitting just below the surface, and at any moment, I might break down in tears.

"No, but thanks," I say as I close the curtains again. "I think I'm going to get dressed and go out. Something about being in my house makes me feel like a sitting duck."

"Aww, Carey. I'm sure it's nothing. Don't be like that.

Take a shower, go out, and enjoy the day. I bet when you get back you'll feel much better about things."

As I walk back to my bedroom, I smile at how supportive Jenna can be. She's a little rough around the edges, but when push comes to shove, she's the kind of friend who's front and center in your corner. I appreciate that, especially after all she's been through.

"I think I will. Thanks for listening to me ramble on like a crazy person. I'm going to grab a shower and then do some shopping. I'll call you later."

"Good. Shopping will take your mind off things. Maybe call Emory. She told me last night she's having no luck at all with any of her work this week. Something about her hands hurting every time she picks up her chisel. I bet she'd love to go browsing for stuff. I'll talk to you later, Carey. Remember, you're strong. Don't let that shithead ex of yours make you feel otherwise."

I chuckle at her description of Chase and end the call. She's right. A letter and a few messages aren't going to make me dissolve into a puddle of tears. He's going to have to do more than that to make me worry.

12

I SEE you finally read my messages. You really should check them more often. It could be life and death, and you'd never even know they were there.

That museum guy wasn't that hard to kill. It's not like he was a bodybuilder or anything like that. Like most egghead types, he was light and easy to lift to the noose. Of course, the drug sneaked into his drink didn't hurt. He didn't make a noise or even move when it was time.

The world isn't going to miss that guy. Seriously, the director of a toy museum? Not exactly a guy who scaled great heights, that one. No wife or girlfriend. Nobody to even care he's gone.

Just another person easily forgotten.

He's the first, but he won't be the last. You probably guessed that already, though. Skinny museum guy was meant as a sign. Did you pick up on that? You should have.

Now it's just a matter of when the next one will

happen. Unsure what this is all about? You should know, but typical Carey is oblivious to what she's done. That's okay. Give it time. You'll understand by the time this is all over.

For now, just know that you're never alone. You think you are, but there are always eyes on you.

To be honest, not striking at you right from the beginning has been difficult. You see, you have it coming. Not sure what that means?

You'll see soon enough.

For now, just know there's a method to this madness. You brought this upon yourself, so no blaming others. It was you who was responsible. You likely can't even remember what you did.

See, that's the thing. You were careless. Still are. That's why you can't fathom why anyone would do this to you. If you think hard enough, you'll remember.

Not to worry. You'll have time to figure it out. Our relationship will eventually come to an end, but there's a timetable to all of this. Surprised to hear we have a relationship? Oh, yes. We have for a while.

You may not think so, though. You have a way of moving on so easily. People admire that, don't they?

Not all people, but most, right?

Still have no clue who this is? Patience. All will be revealed in due time.

For now, the letter should give you some clues. You're a smart girl. You'll figure it out. That's what people always say, isn't it? But you're wondering if you'll ever get the answers you want.

Rest assured, all your questions will be answered by the end of this.

Are you enjoying your time off work? Is it like a vacation, or has the death of that toy guy made your life miserable?

It's about to get much worse, though. That's a warning, if you choose to take it.

So why is this happening to you? You've asked yourself that so many times, haven't you? It's striking you can't figure this out. You like to think of yourself as a thoughtful person. Are you, though? Really?

You smiled at that old lady on the way up the stairs after you took your trash down to the dumpster the other night. Do you think that makes you kind? Why didn't you stop to talk to her? She certainly appeared lonely and would have probably loved to talk.

Then there was the man at the grocery store you let get ahead of you in line because he only had a handful of items. That seems like something a thoughtful, nice person would do. That makes you a good person, right?

See, that's not really enough. Basic civility doesn't equal goodness.

So what's going to happen now? Well, you'll continue to get clues about what all this is about. More people will have to die, of course. As you well know, people don't tend to get the message if you just tell them what's on your mind. They need something more, something to force their eyes open, before they truly understand.

In the meantime, I'll be watching you. I like keeping an eye on you. Yes, your life is a bit boring, but I have a plan to make it more exciting.

Are you ready?

Buckle up. Things are about to get even more interesting. The race is on to see who will win.

Will it be you who figures out who I am before it's too late? My bet is no, but I hope you try your best.

Isn't that what a good person always does?

13

THREE HOURS of shopping results in a brand new black dress and the cutest black shoes with a low heel and bows on the top. I return to my apartment complex happier than I've felt in days, pleased that I didn't let what happened this morning make me hide out in my bedroom for the entire day.

The four teenage boys from that family are awake and outside wreaking havoc. Why the school district allows those parents to homeschool those delinquents is beyond me. I'd bet they sleep until nearly twelve, so when do they get any education in if they're outside causing trouble by mid-afternoon?

I watch them for a few seconds as I sit in my car and then head upstairs to my apartment. I should anonymously report that family. As soon as that thought enters my head, I dismiss it. I'm not the type of person to snitch on people, even if they are a menace to the neighborhood.

As I walk up the stairs, I silently wish I could, though.

Something tells me those boys are headed for disaster as adults.

God help us all if and when that happens.

I reach the second floor, and just as I'm sliding my key into the lock, a loud crash startles me. I spin around to look for what made that terrible noise but see nothing. It sounded like a metal garbage can being slammed against the floor or wall, but I see no can and no one who may have thrown anything.

God, my mind is starting to play tricks on me.

It's that letter. I'd put it out of my mind while I was out shopping, but now that I'm back here at my apartment, the uneasy feeling it gave me when I read it has come back with a vengeance.

To myself, I mumble as I open the door, "Calm down, Carey. You're letting your imagination run wild again. Someone dropped something. That's all. Just relax."

That's enough to get my focus back, so I get inside my apartment and slam the door behind me. Tossing my new dress and shoes on the sofa, I head to the kitchen to get a drink of water, but my phone begins to vibrate in my purse and I pull it out.

I see it's a number from the museum, so I quickly answer it. Michael Tanner's voice in my ear cheers me up instantly.

"Hi, Carey. I'm calling to let you know the police are done with the storage room upstairs, so we can get back to work. I'm going to have everyone come back on Monday. By the way, there's going to be a memorial service for Randall this Friday night here at the museum. It seems right to do it here. If you'd like to say a few words, just let me know. No pressure, though. I know this has been tough for you, so nobody expects you to do anything."

My initial happiness at hearing I'll be able to return to work is dimmed a bit as I listen to Michael talk about the memorial service. Not that I don't think Mr. James deserves one. Of course, he does. I just don't know if I have it in me to stand up in front of everyone and talk about how much I'm going to miss him.

"Oh, okay. I'm so happy we'll be back to work come next week. I've been going a bit stir crazy here in my apartment."

Michael laughs and says, "Oh, I know what you mean. My wife told me in no uncertain terms this morning that I needed to get out of the house, so naturally, I came into the office."

I chuckle, even as I wonder what office he means. He must mean the office Mr. James used to occupy, of course, but I can't say that doesn't feel strange. I know it's only right, although it feels like jumping into his seat while it's still warm.

What was that thing my mother used to always say? Something about taking her seat?

It comes to me only a moment later. Would you jump in my grave that fast?

"So I'll send you the details of the memorial service in an email since I know I'll forget something important if I try to give you all of them over the phone. It's not going to be anything big. Randall wouldn't want that. Just something to let us pay our respects and say goodbye to the director who did so much for this museum in the time he was here."

As with every other time I think about my boss being gone, a heaviness comes over me. I nod as Michael explains about the service, but all I can think is I still can't believe Mr. James is gone.

"Okay. Thank you, Michael. Do you need me to do anything to help you?"

I don't mention that I mean at the job and not for the memorial service because I don't want to sound callous. It's just that I don't think I can do much if I'm falling apart every few minutes.

Thankfully, he says he doesn't need help. "Misha is here, so she's handling a lot of things. I want to make sure she doesn't feel left out on a limb since I'm going to be the interim director."

"Oh, yes. I understand. Misha has been so wonderful all these years as your assistant."

Suddenly, I begin to wonder if he's going to want her to work for him while he's director. I'm not sure where that will leave me, though.

As if he's reading my mind, Michael says, "Please don't worry, Carey. Your job is secure. Nobody, and that includes you and Misha, will be doing anything you haven't always done. It's only the person at the top who's changing, and that's only for a short time."

Curious if he's looking to replace Mr. James, I ask, "Will you be going for the director job once it's posted?"

In truth, it's only natural that the board of directors of the museum would consider Michael first. He's been the assistant director, so to move him into the director's position would mean almost no upheaval in the office. Things would continue along just as they'd always been. The transition would be smooth, and the museum would run like it had under Mr. James.

Michael doesn't answer for a few seconds, but then says with a laugh, "My wife has asked me that half a dozen times in the past few days. Honestly, I don't know. I love where I'm at here. Not that I couldn't do the director's job, but it's a lot more work."

"Well, I think you'd be great at it, not that you asked my opinion. Whatever you decide, I know you'll have the best interest of the museum in mind."

I can hear the smile in his voice when he says, "Thank you, Carey. Randall always said you were the most supportive assistant he ever had, so I appreciate that."

For a moment, I consider asking when my boss said that, but I don't want to sound like I'm fishing for compliments. It's just that Mr. James never said anything like that to me.

"Well, thank you, Michael. I care about my job and the museum, so whatever I can do to help you, just let me know."

After saying he will, he adds, "I need to call everyone else now, so I hope you won't mind me flying. I guess I could have done this all through one email to everyone on staff, but I felt like this needed to be more personal. I'll see you Friday?"

"Oh, yes. Let me know if you need anything from me before then."

When the call ends, I sit down on the sofa next to my new dress and shoes I'll be wearing to the service. I guess it's fortunate I fell in love with a black dress today. In the back of my mind, I was probably thinking this new dress would be for my boss's funeral. It's odd that I haven't heard anything about that, but maybe there won't be one and the memorial service will be the only way we'll be able to say goodbye.

Sadness washes over me at the thought that Mr. James had nobody in his life to arrange a funeral so instead all he gets is a memorial service from his coworkers. Whatever he was outside of work, he deserves a proper goodbye.

Then something occurs to me. Why isn't anyone in his circle of friends doing anything? Perhaps I'll ask Nicholas when he calls later. He may not have truly been a friend of Mr. James, but he must know others who were closer to him.

Lost in thought about his life outside of work, I'm interrupted by a knock on my door. Instantly, every muscle in my body tenses, and my heart begins to race.

I stare at the door, unsure if I want to answer it knowing there's a chance it could be Chase, but a second knock makes me think I can't avoid opening my front door. If it's my ex, then I'll have to deal with him.

My hands shaking, I walk over to the door and look out the peephole to see that policeman who spent all that time questioning me at the museum that day. What is Officer Thompson doing here?

Slowly, I open the door and give the officer a smile. "Hello, again."

"Hello, Miss Mitchell. Do you have some time to talk to me? I have some more questions I need to ask you."

His statement confuses me. What else could he possibly have to ask me?

"Oh, really? What about?"

He smiles, but it never reaches his eyes. "About the murder of your boss, Randall James. May I come in?"

Even though I guess I could refuse to allow him entrance to my apartment, I step back to open the door wider to let him in. I have nothing to fear speaking to him, so why not? I've done nothing wrong.

Officer Thompson looks around when he stops a few feet into my home, and I suddenly feel very exposed. I'm not sure why, though.

Walking past him to sit on the sofa, I ask, "What can I help with? Have you gotten any leads as to who did that to Mr. James?"

The officer doesn't sit down, so when he looks at me, I feel like he's standing in judgment over me. He takes his tiny notebook out of his shirt pocket and clicks the end of his pen, a routine I bet he's done a thousand times.

He reads over his notes before looking down at me. His voice as serious as his expression, he says, "We've been told you were the last person to see Mr. James. Is that true?"

"I'm not sure. I did see him after the benefit in one of the collection rooms, but I don't know if he spoke to anyone after we finished talking," I answer, hoping he sees I'm being honest.

The officer nods and writes something in his notebook before returning his focus to me. "Well, we haven't found anyone who spoke to him after you. In fact, we've been told by several people who were there that night that you and Mr. James argued. Can you tell me what that was about?"

I stare at him stunned at his characterization of any conversation my boss and I had that night. "I think you've been given some incorrect information. Mr. James and I never argued. We simply didn't have that kind of relationship."

Officer Thompson arches his right eyebrow like he doesn't believe what I just said and jots something in his notebook. When he finishes, he looks up at me and asks, "Then what kind of relationship did you have?"

What does that mean?

"I don't think I like what you're implying," I say, already tired of this man and his attitude.

He's as defiant as I am, though, and continues. "I'm not implying anything, Miss Mitchell. I simply asked what kind of relationship you had with Mr. James."

My heart slams into my chest as I suppress the urge to order him to leave my apartment at once. "A professional one. He was my boss. I was his executive assistant. That's it. We didn't know anything about one another outside of the museum. For God's sake, I just found out in the past few days that he was a widower after his wife died of cancer."

I don't know why, but just saying that makes me want to cry. I refuse to do that in front of the police, though, so I turn away and walk into the kitchen to get a glass of water. Not interested in Officer Thompson staying any longer than he has to, I don't offer him one.

Of course, he follows me, and when I turn around, he's leaning on my counter practically studying me. I don't know if I'm acting guilty right now. Maybe I am. I do feel somewhat guilty about not knowing my boss lost his wife while I was working as his assistant. Did I miss the signs that he was in mourning, or did he hide it so well like he did everything else in his private life that I wouldn't have been able to tell?

Either way, whatever this cop thinks he's doing here, I'm not happy about it.

"Are you okay, Miss Mitchell? You seem overwrought."

His tone irritates me, as does his use of the word overwrought. Does he plan to say I'm hysterical next? Typical man in power.

After taking a big gulp of water, I look him squarely in the eyes and answer, "I'm sad about the man I worked for being killed, and I'm still dealing with being the one who found him. Perhaps you might keep that in mind as you ask me these questions. I've got feelings, and although that may make me seem overwrought to you, it's perfectly normal."

Surprisingly, that seems to affect him, and his entire demeanor changes. He sighs heavily and stands up straight, almost as if he finally realizes he was being disrespectful before.

"Yes, I do understand. I'm sorry for your loss. I am. I simply need to do my job to find out who murdered Mr. James."

His change brings about one in me also, and I smile, hoping to ease the tension between us. "I appreciate that. I hope you find whoever did that to him and put them away forever. Whatever else Mr. James may have been at the museum, he was a man who cared deeply about the collections we offer and wanted more than anything else to show the world that toys have more meaning than being simple child's playthings. Mr. James deserved so much better than he got from whoever thought it was okay to take his life."

As I speak, he nods like he agrees, but it feels hollow, as if he's trying to placate me. When I finish, he barely spends enough time taking a breath before continuing his questioning.

"So you're saying you and Mr. James did not argue Friday night at the benefit the museum held?"

I know I should just admit what he said about Nicholas, but I can't find the words to explain the context properly, mostly because I don't understand why he would say that myself. So I shake my head and hope the officer moves on to something else before the look on my face makes him think I'm lying.

Which I guess I am, technically. Or maybe it's a sin of omission. I just don't think it's germane to the case. My boss's opinion on his friend possibly being interested in me has nothing to do with why anyone would kill him.

Even though I have absolutely no idea why Mr. James even said anything at all.

Lost in thought about that cryptic warning of his, I don't hear Officer Thompson ask me something until the last few words are coming out of his mouth and he's staring at me like he expects an answer.

"I'm sorry. I missed much of what you said."

That expectation of his becomes more intense, and he

repeats his question. "Do you know why anyone would think you and your boss argued that night?"

I shrug and answer, "No. You'd have to ask them."

He flips through his notebook and stops a few pages back before looking at me again. "Funny you should say that. I did ask the two people who told me you and Mr. James had a disagreement, and they each said they saw you talking to a man before your boss and you argued. Ring any bells?"

Even though this is my apartment, I suddenly feel trapped like an animal in a cage. So someone saw me with Nicholas and then likely saw Mr. James's disapproval and jumped to the conclusion that we disagreed about it. I wonder who did that? Two people? I can't imagine who, but then again, I wasn't paying attention to who was watching me that night.

Odd that anyone was. I'm not generally the center of attention.

Again, I shake my head. "Nope. I talked to a few people that night, including my boss. He tended to be a bit of a fusspot when it came to charity events. He always wanted to make sure everything was perfect so donors would want to be generous. That's unfortunately a big part of the director's job."

The officer nods and writes some part of what I say in his notebook. "Hmmm. Perhaps that's what these people were interpreting as arguing."

"Who were the people who said that?"

Now it's his turn to not want to answer a question. "I'm sorry. I can't divulge that."

I take that as my cue to escort him to the door, so I

begin walking away as I say, "Well, I don't think I can provide anything more that could help. I didn't see Mr. James much that night, and when I did, we didn't argue."

Unfortunately, he doesn't take the hint. Instead, he simply turns around in the spot he's claimed in my kitchen and asks, "I have other questions."

A tiny bit of hate flashes inside me for this man, but I stuff it down and paste a smile on my face. "Oh yes? About what?"

"Nicholas Madera."

I want to make a smart ass crack like, "Oh? Is he dead too?" but I refrain from that and continue to smile as I say, "I can't tell you much about him either. We only met at the benefit."

"I've been told that you're seeing him now."

"Is that a crime?" I ask, close to telling Officer Thompson he needs to leave and not return unless he wants to deal with my lawyer.

Except I don't have a lawyer and can't afford to hire one.

"He and Mr. James were friends, I'm told. Is that true?"

I open the door, done with this man and his stupid questions. "I think that's something you'd want to ask the man himself. I need to get on with my day, so you'll have to excuse me, Officer Thompson."

This time he takes the hint and begins to walk toward the door. When he reaches me, he stops and says, "Thank you for your time, Miss Mitchell. I may have more questions to ask as the investigation continues."

That's it. I'm fed up with this man and his questions.

"Officer, I've told you all I know. I can't imagine this is how actual murder investigations go. I'm a relatively small woman, as you can clearly see. I couldn't hurt anyone, much less a grown man, and even if I could, I wouldn't be able to hang him from the ceiling. I don't know why you're so misguided when it comes to me, but I was merely an executive assistant to Mr. James. I sincerely hope you find the person who did this, but I don't think that's going to happen if you keep talking to me."

My statement seems to take him by surprise, and for a few moments, he doesn't respond. Not that I need him to say anything else. Every word out of this man's mouth bothers me, and if I never had to speak to him again in this lifetime, I'd be thrilled.

When he regains his composure, he says, "By the way. It wouldn't have taken anyone strong to kill Mr. James. He was strangled. I'm assuming it happened at the benefit, in fact."

I feel my eyes grow wide in shock at what he says. Strangled? Someone got that close to Mr. James to strangle him and then hung him from the ceiling?

He doesn't say anything else before walking out the door. As I close it behind him, I can't help but think there was much more to my boss's personal life I didn't know.

My hands shaking, I lock the deadbolt and walk to my bedroom as the thought of someone intentionally plotting to kill Mr. James fills my mind. Why would anyone want to do that?

14

After taking a four hour nap, I wake up to see it's already dark out. Instantly, I regret wasting so much of my day and put the blame squarely where it belongs.

That ridiculous cop bothering me with his asinine questions.

I can't imagine how they expect to catch the killer when they're pestering me. Even if I could have easily strangled Mr. James, which I doubt I could accomplish on my own, how the hell could I get his body lifted high enough to suspend him from the ceiling?

It's clear to me they should be looking for at least one man. No woman my size could pick up a grown man. What on earth are they teaching cops in whatever school they attend to learn how to investigate?

Scrubbing the last of my nap from my eyes, I roll out of bed and make my way out to the kitchen to get a drink. I gulp down two big glasses of iced tea and then head back to my room, but out of the corner of my eye, I see something on the floor near the door.

My heart skips a beat as I turn to look at it. Just like the other day, it's a white envelope. My mind fills with a single sentence repeating over and over.

Please don't let it be another one of those letters.

I want to walk over there and prove my thoughts wrong. I can't move, though. It's like my feet are encased in concrete, and I'm stuck here in the tiny hallway between my kitchen and my bedroom.

Maybe I should have told Officer Thompson about the first one. I know Jenna said not to tell the police, but now that I've gotten two of them, I think I need to.

Oh, God. Why is this happening to me?

I want to believe it's Chase trying to scare me so I'll come running back to him. It seems like something he would do. I wouldn't put it past him.

Yet as much as I try to convince myself it has to be my ex-boyfriend, I'm not able to actually believe that. He's never been one to do much with actual letters. I don't know if I ever saw him handwrite anything in all the time we were together. If the messages were coming by text, I'd definitely be able to see him being behind them, but writing a letter and using an envelope feels wrong for him.

Oh God! Is it possible I have two different crazy people threatening me, my ex and whoever's writing these damn letters and the online messages?

I'm finally able to move my feet, so I slowly approach the envelope slipped under my front door. It looks perfectly innocent just sitting there on the floor. In a time long gone by, a letter secretly left for a young woman might be something intensely romantic, a gift someone like me would relish.

All I feel when I look at it now, though, is dread.

My stomach tightens into a knot, and by the time I'm standing above the envelope, I feel like I'm going to be sick. Never before in my life has anything terrified me as much as the slip of paper I know is inside.

As my hands tremble, I steel myself for what I'm about to read. Suddenly, that chant from when I was a little girl begins to play in my head. Sticks and stones may break my bones, but words can never hurt me. It's stupid, but by the fifth time it repeats, I begin to feel a little better.

Words definitely can hurt, but I don't want to think about that right now. Nothing in that letter is going to actually cause me harm. I need to remember that.

I take a deep breath and say in a low voice, "Okay, I can do this. It's just a piece of paper. It's just someone playing a prank on me."

For a long moment, I stare at the envelope and try to convince myself this isn't anything important. A piece of paper can't hurt me.

Crouching down, I touch the envelope as my heart slams into my chest. It's smooth against my fingertips, and I grab the edge between my thumb and forefinger. When I lift it up to see if there's writing on it, I see nothing.

A thought flashes through my mind that maybe this isn't meant for me. It doesn't have my name on it. It could be for anyone living on my floor or even anyone living in this building, for that matter.

That calms me for long enough that I can stand up without my legs giving out. I flip the envelope over and see no writing on the back either.

Even as I wish I could believe this isn't for me, I know better. Maybe if it was the first one I might be able to convince myself it's for someone else or just some junk mail like those menus restaurants routinely leave in my mailbox.

But it's not. That's how I know the letter inside is meant for me.

I slowly back away from my door as I clutch the white envelope in my right hand, staring at it the entire time as I move toward my living room couch. The coolness is gone now, replaced by the sweat from my palm.

I clip the corner of my coffee table with my calf and let out a loud cry while pain shoots up behind my right knee. Tumbling backwards, I fall onto the couch, a nervous wreck at what I'm about to read and in agony as my leg begins to ache all the way down to my ankle.

"Son of a bitch!"

In pain, I throw the envelope onto the cushion while I rub my leg. Just what I needed today. What else can go wrong?

When I feel a little better, I can't avoid seeing my poison pen letter sitting there in front of me just waiting to be opened. I should just tear it up and throw it into the garbage. That's what I ought to do.

I won't, though.

Still hurting and now angry, I grab the envelope and shake it. "So you think you're going to terrorize me today? Forget it! You're some words on a piece of paper. That's all. Nothing more. So don't think you're going to ruin my damn day."

If only I meant any of that.

I can't hold off anymore, so I give the envelope one last angry glare and slide my finger under the flap to open it. Before I slip the piece of paper out, I silently promise myself I'm not going to fall apart, no matter what the note says.

"Here goes nothing."

With my hand shaking, I pull out the letter and unfold it. The horrible words stare back at me, practically cutting through me like a hot knife through butter. Cruel words about no one missing Mr. James now that he's gone because he meant nothing to the world.

Then it says his death was a sign. What does that mean? A sign of what?

My heart clenches when I then read, "You're never alone." They say there are always eyes on me. I don't understand. Why is this happening?

I can't read anymore. It's too much.

Setting the letter on the coffee table, I close my eyes so I don't have to look at it. It's too ugly, too horrible to read.

But I know I have to, so after a few minutes, I open my eyes and lean forward to snatch it off the table. I'm a mixture of terrified and angry while I begin to scan the letter again and see the person behind it say I brought this on myself.

How is that possible? I'm no one. I go to work five days a week and then come home. My life is as mundane as they come. Even more, I'm a good person. I always let people cut in front of me at the grocery store when they have fewer items than I do. I hold the door for people whenever there's someone behind me. I thank cashiers with a smile when they hand me my receipts. Why would anyone want to do this to me?

Whoever this madman is, they think I'm going to be able to figure out clues in these letters. I don't know why they think that. They say we have a relationship. That's not possible. No one I know would be so cruel.

I toss the letter away onto the table and sit back against the sofa. Mr. James died because of me. Now I know that for sure.

But why? And more people will die?

My breath catches in my chest at the thought that someone I care about will be the next victim. Why is this happening? What does it have to do with me? Why would this person hurt anyone I know?

I don't know what to do. Should I call the police? I have no interest in dealing with that horrible Officer Thompson again. He'll probably say I'm to blame for Mr. James being strangled because of this letter.

My apartment suddenly doesn't feel safe anymore. The person behind these notes killed my boss, and now he's threatening to kill someone else. Will it be me?

I rush into my bedroom and grab my phone off the nightstand. Emory will know what to do. She's always so cool-headed about things. The way she handled finding Mr. James while I unraveled like a cheap suit shows that.

She answers on the third ring, and while normally that would tell me she's busy with her art, I can't think about that right now. She'll just have to forgive me for interrupting her.

"Hey, Carey! What's going on?" she chirps out, unaware my life is spiraling down into madness.

"Emory, I need your help! I got another one of those letters today, and I don't think it's Chase. Oh, God! I'm so scared!"

Every word tumbles out of my mouth like they're desperate for someone to hear them. I hold back the tears that want to come, desperate to not seem like I'm falling apart, even if I am.

"What? Calm down. It's going to be okay. Anyone who'd threaten you in a letter isn't going to do anything. They're cowards. Just remember that," she says with so much confidence I want to believe her.

But she hasn't heard what the letter said. When she does, she'll know it's bad.

"They didn't threaten me this time. They threatened…"

I stop because I don't exactly know how to finish that sentence. Emory waits a second or two for me to start talking again, but I don't know how to explain it.

"The letter didn't threaten you? Well, that's good! Then you're in the clear."

As I begin to nervously pace back and forth across the living room, I shake my head at her unwarranted optimism. "No, you don't understand. The letter threatened others. It said that my boss wasn't the last one to die. It said just wait until I see who's next. Emory, I'm freaking out here! What if someone I care about is in danger? I don't know what to do."

She doesn't immediately answer, which upsets me even more. Why isn't she saying anything?

Finally, I ask, "Are you still there?"

"Yeah, yeah. I'm thinking. I still don't buy that anyone is going to actually get hurt, Carey. Are we thinking this person is taking responsibility for your boss's death?"

"Yeah, I think so."

Emory doesn't miss a beat this time. "Then you have to tell the cops. They're conducting a murder investigation, and this seems like evidence. Give it to them and let them handle it."

"But what about someone I know getting hurt? I'd hate it if you or Jenna had anything happen to you because this person wants to torment me. Oh, God! I wish I knew who was behind all of this. It's twisted. I don't understand why they're doing this."

"Calm down. Call the cops and tell them you've been getting these letters. They'll know what to do."

Dread fills me at the mere thought of talking to Officer Thompson again. He already thinks I'm guilty of something, although I don't understand why. What if he twists this to make it look like I killed Mr. James?

"Okay. Thanks, Emory."

"It's going to be okay," she says in her sweetest voice she only uses when someone is really down. "Just call the police and let them handle it."

"I will. Thanks. Do me a favor, though."

I don't say what I want her to do because I'm afraid if I put it out there into the universe, it'll be real. She waits for me to continue before asking, "What? Do you need me to come over? I will, if you want. My muse is back, but she's being a bit of a bitch, so I haven't gotten much done."

"No, no. I'm okay. I just want you to be careful, okay? I know you aren't freaked out by these letters like I am, but I'm worried now. I don't want anything to happen to you."

Emory laughs, as if there's anything amusing about being worried your friend is going to be killed. "I thought you didn't get scared."

"Well, I am now! Stop laughing about this. I'm really upset."

"Okay. I'm sorry. I didn't mean to laugh. I'm not making fun of you. Honest. I promise to be careful. I'll even look both ways when I cross the street, which you know is something I never do."

She never does. It's the most irrational thing I've ever seen. Emory routinely walks out into the crosswalk without even giving a second thought about cars coming at her. It's insane.

"That's only because you want someone to hit you so you can have a big payday when you sue them."

For a second time, she laughs. "True, but I promise I'll look from now on until this is all settled. Don't worry, Carey. Letter writers are cowards. They don't have the balls to say what they have to say to your face or even call you on the phone. Cowards. Let me know what the cops say."

I slow my pacing down to a leisurely walk and take a deep breath in, letting it out in a rush. "I will."

Even I can hear the lack of conviction in my words as I say that.

My friend picks up on it immediately and says, "You

are going to call them, aren't you? This isn't something you can handle by yourself, Carey."

"I know. I know," I say, sighing. "It's just that Officer Thompson was here earlier, and he told me my boss was strangled before he was hanged. I think he believes I did it, Emory. Why would he think that?"

"What makes you say he thinks you did it? Everyone who knows you knows you couldn't do that to anyone. Not even Mr. James, and that guy was a pain in the ass on his best days to you."

I don't know how to explain it, but I know that cop thinks I had some part in my boss's death. Why, I have no idea, but he does.

"It's the way he says things when he interviews me. I nearly broke down in tears the last time."

"Then when you call, ask to speak to someone else. It's not like he's the only person on the planet who can help you. Remember, they're supposed to serve and protect, not upset you. Keep that in mind, okay?"

God, Emory is so much stronger than I am. I can imagine her calling the police and telling them in no uncertain terms she wants nothing to do with Officer Thompson. They'd listen to her too. Something in the way she speaks in that authoritative tone always makes people do what she wants.

"I will. Okay, I'm going to call them right now. Thanks, Emory. I'll let you know what they say."

"Good luck, honey. Call me as soon as you're done talking to them."

"But what if you're working? I don't want to interrupt your muse again."

She huffs her disgust and answers, "Fuck her. She should want to come when I need her. I don't eat means she dies, so she better get that straight right here and now. Call me and let me know what happened with the cops. And remember, don't take any shit from them or anyone else. They're supposed to help, so make sure they do."

Leave it to Emory to tell off her muse and suggest my doing the same with the police all in one conversation.

"I will. Thanks!"

When I get off the phone with her, I start pacing again, nervous about calling the police. Do I call 9-1-1? This isn't an emergency technically, so is that the wrong number to call? Jesus, I hate this. I want to go back to my life that didn't include knowing the right way to call the police about being harassed through letters.

After ten more minutes of pacing while my mind played tug-of-war over how to call the police or if I should just go to the police station, I finally press 9-1-1 on my cell and hope I don't get yelled at for using it for non-emergency purposes.

"9-1-1, where is your emergency?" a woman's voice asks, instantly making me feel like I've done the wrong thing.

"Uh, the Brightline Apartments, Building C, Apartment 2C," I answer hesitantly.

I consider adding that it isn't really an emergency and I just need to speak to the police, but before I can, the woman asks, "What's your emergency?"

With even more hesitation, I hem and haw for a few seconds before saying, "I just need the police. I'm receiving threatening letters and don't know what to do. I'm scared."

I wait for her to reprimand me for abusing 9-1-1, but the woman kindly says, "Okay, what's your name?"

"Carey Mitchell," I answer, more relieved than I've felt in days.

"Okay, Miss Mitchell. I'm going to send this report on, and the police will get in touch with you soon. Are you in danger now?"

That's a loaded question. I honestly don't know how to answer it.

"I don't know. I'm in my apartment, and the door's locked, but I truly don't know if I'm in danger or not. I woke up and found this threatening letter slipped under my door."

"Okay, I'm including that in what I'm sending to the police. Until they get there, stay in with the door locked. Don't open it for anyone but the police, just in case. Do you need an ambulance?"

I smile, thankful I don't need that kind of help. "No, I'm okay. Just really scared."

"Well, Miss Mitchell, just stay inside safe and sound and the police will get to you soon."

Before she ends the call, I quickly say, "Thank you for your help and not being upset it's not really an emergency. I appreciate that."

"You're welcome. Remember, stay inside your apartment until the police arrive."

"I will."

Happy I actually called for help, I set my phone down on my kitchen counter and let out a heavy sigh of relief. I know I probably have a good wait until the police come by since I'm not really in danger at the moment, but it's a good feeling knowing I'll ultimately get to tell an officer about what's been going on.

When I hear a knock on my front door ten minutes later, I freeze in place, sure it can't be the police yet. I stare at the door, silently wishing whoever it is will just go away.

The knocking stops momentarily, but only a few seconds afterward, it starts up again. I can't move I'm so terrified.

God, just go away!

Then a man's voice says, "Miss Mitchell, it's the police. Are you in there?"

Thrilled to hear help has arrived, I rush over to the door and throw it open. My happiness is dashed when I see the last person in the world I want to talk to right now.

15

"The dispatcher said you called about someone threatening you?" Officer Thompson says with nothing but doubt filling his voice as he stares blankly at me.

Why on earth is he here? He's not going to be helpful at all.

I don't invite him in because of all the police officers in this town, he's the only one I really don't want to deal with about this issue. Why didn't they send someone else? Is this guy the only person who answers calls?

Looking around him for another officer I might be able to deal with, all I see is that guy who lives two doors down who every weekend cooks the stinkiest food I've ever had the misfortune to smell. He gives me a look like he's curious about why a cop is at my door talking to me, and all I can muster is a sad smile.

"Miss Mitchell, did you call 9-1-1 about someone threatening you?"

I return my focus to Officer Thompson and sigh in

utter frustration. "Yes. I called because I received a threatening letter. Is there no one else on the police force in this town? Aren't you investigating a murder? How do you have time to chase down reports of threats to random women?"

He smiles, and as much as I hate to admit it, he's a very handsome man when he's not interrogating someone. That doesn't change the fact that I don't want to talk to him about my problem. I don't know why, but he's going to twist everything I say. I just know it.

"My job as an officer isn't restricted to only investigating a single case. When I heard it was you calling about being threatened, I wanted to come back here and see if you're okay."

"I'm fine. Thank you. Perhaps I'll just wait for another officer. You don't work around the clock, do you?"

Again, he smiles, but this time my question makes him laugh. "No, but you're going to have to settle for me on this. I assure you I want to help, so if you'll just let me in, we can talk."

About my boss being murdered, which this man thinks I could easily do. He's probably decided I'm guilty already.

We stand there in my doorway practically staring one another down for what feels like forever until I finally give in and step back so he can come inside. If I wasn't truly worried about these ominous letters, I would have politely told him no thank you and goodbye.

As I slowly close my front door, I remind myself that I need to channel Emory when it comes to Officer Thompson. No pushing me around this time. The moment he starts in with his accusatory looks and comments about Mr. James's death, I'll be ordering him to leave.

I walk past him leaning against the island in my kitchen and can't believe this guy is so comfortable in my house. I should offer him something to drink since it's hot out today, but I don't want him to get the idea I'm happy to see him.

After I grab a bottle of water, I stand in front of the refrigerator, sure I look like the polar opposite of him as I fidget with taking the cap off and then twist it back on. I swear to God I've never been this nervous around a police officer before.

Then again, I've never personally known someone who was murdered. These past few days have seen a lot of firsts for me.

"So tell me about this threat, Miss Mitchell," my least favorite cop says to begin our conversation.

Is that smugness I hear under his words? Why would he act like that? I'm an upstanding, law-abiding citizen of this town. Don't I deserve the same respect everyone else gets?

"It's two actually," I say before taking a swig of water.

He writes something in that little notebook of his and then lifts his head to look at me. "Two? Both today?"

Why do I get the feeling he's not taking this seriously? What kind of question is that? Who sends two threatening letters in one day?

Biting my tongue so I don't ask any of those questions, I level my gaze on him and refrain from rolling my eyes.

"No, not two today. I received one the other day and one today. And some messages on social media."

Nothing in my tone says I appreciate any of this, and I see by the surprised expression that comes over him that he isn't used to people actually pushing back on his rudeness. Or his idiocy. I'm not sure which is more off-putting.

"Do you still have them? The letters, I mean," he asks, and I notice his tone of voice is softer now.

I nod and blow the air out of my mouth, tired of all of this. "Hang on. I'll go get the first one."

As I walk away toward my bedroom, he calls after me, "Why didn't you call 9-1-1 after you received the first threatening letter?"

Not bothering to look back at him because I'm sure I'm going to say something I don't want to if I see some smug expression on his face, I answer, "Because I didn't think it was worthy of calling the cops."

Instead of simply waiting for me to return in a few seconds, he continues to talk loudly. "Any time you feel like you aren't safe, you can call the police, Miss Mitchell. We're here to protect and serve."

Under my breath, I mumble as I grab the letter off my nightstand, "Really? I thought your job was to hassle and make people feel bad after their bosses are murdered."

When I return to the kitchen, I hand him the first letter and then walk into the living room to get the second one. Now that he has the two of them, he sets them both down on the counter and reads them, taking notes in his little pad regarding when I received them and what the threats are.

I don't say anything as he studies them but think to

myself there's no way it's Chase. He's just not a letter writing kind of person. Texts, yeah. Phone calls, sure. But these letters aren't from him. Plus, they aren't written in his handwriting, which I remember being particularly awful.

Finally, Officer Thompson nods and turns to look at me. "I'm sorry if you feel like I'm being difficult with you, Miss Mitchell. I was simply doing my job by coming here the other day to talk to you."

"Maybe if you didn't make every conversation seem like an interrogation I wouldn't feel that way."

Wow. I've never been that forthright with anyone in my life. I really must be channeling Emory. Good. I have a feeling Officer Thompson hasn't had enough people tell him how damn officious he is.

His eyes open wide at my scolding, but he doesn't say anything in response. Perhaps he'll leave now and give my little case to another officer.

Unfortunately, he doesn't make any moves toward the door, which means he's staying.

"What do you think the person who sent the first letter meant by they know you're relieved Mr. James is dead and he got what he deserved?"

God, why does everything he says sound like a goddamned indictment of me?

"I don't know," I say as I struggle not to cry. It's pure frustration, but I just know he'll think it's evidence of my being guilty.

"You said that you and your boss had nothing but a work relationship. Could this be from someone at the museum who knows he drove you crazy? It sounds like the person knows firsthand how much you had to deal with from Mr. James."

I swear to God this man has already decided I'm the murderer. He's officer, judge, and jury all rolled up into one infuriating package.

"What makes you think my boss drove me crazy? I never said that. Who said that to you? Was it someone at the museum?"

All those questions only make me look guilty, or guiltier as far as Officer Thompson is concerned, but I can't stop myself. I want to know who said that.

Of course, he can't divulge that information. Why, I have no idea. Does he think I'm going to go on a vindictive rampage at work if I know who said Mr. James drove me crazy? If he had any idea of what kind of person I am, he'd know I couldn't even eat someone's lunch out of the staff refrigerator without feeling bad, much less kill someone.

Regardless of how crazy he made me.

"A number of your co-workers told me that Mr. James was a difficult man to work for and they didn't think they would have been able to handle it as well as you did," he answers with a smile.

I'm so tired of talking about my boss. It feels wrong to say he was a nightmare to work with sometimes, but he was. But isn't that being disrespectful of the dead?

I hang my head and say, "Mr. James wasn't a bad person. He cared tremendously for the museum. Because of that, he could be difficult, at times."

When Officer Thompson doesn't say anything, I lift my

head and add, "But that doesn't mean he drove me crazy. I was his assistant. That meant everything he wanted to happen at the museum involved me. Some days he could be challenging. Yes, that's the proper word. Challenging. But he didn't deserve to die, and I had nothing to do with it. However, it seems after today's letter that the person behind these threats did. Even worse, he's coming after me."

Officer Thompson shakes his head as I finish talking. "I don't think you're in any real danger. Letter writers like this don't tend to follow through on their threats. They want to scare people. That's their end game, not actually do any physical harm."

I slump over the island, exhausted by all of this. "Now you sound like my friend. She said the same thing. Do you know how terrifying it is to know someone was right outside my door and slipped that note into my apartment, my home where I live? I'm scared to death every time I walk into my living room that there will be another envelope waiting for me."

My emotional outburst doesn't seem to even register with the policeman, and he quickly asks, "Do you have any guess who could be behind these letters?"

Standing up straight, I shake my head. "No. I first thought it might be my ex-boyfriend since he's called me nearly nonstop since I broke up with him, but none of this sounds like him. That's not his handwriting, and to be honest, I don't think he would ever dream of writing an actual letter like this. Chase is more of a hassle someone through the phone kind of person."

"Has he been hassling you over the phone recently?"

the officer asks, jotting down a note about my ex and me breaking up.

"Yes. Well, not really. It's nothing. He just wants to get back together, and I don't. That's it."

I don't know how we got to talking about Chase, but he's not the person who killed Mr. James and he's not the person sending me threatening letters. It's just not his style. My ex is a pest. He's not a murderer.

"So you don't think he could be the person behind these letters. Is there anyone else you can think of who would want to do this to you?"

On the verge of tears because Officer Thompson doesn't seem to be connecting the dots, even though that's literally the main part of his job in a murder investigation, I shake my head. "No. Well, actually, yes. It's the person who murdered my boss! He says it right in the second letter. Why aren't you focusing on that?"

In a calm voice that makes me want to strangle him, he answers, "Because I don't have any idea who it may be."

"Well, from what they said in that second letter, they're planning to become a serial killer. I'd rather not have anyone else I know get murdered or myself, for that matter, so I hope you can figure out who killed my boss and who's threatening me since it's quite clear they're one in the same."

With that, I drink down the rest of my water and walk over to the garbage to throw out the empty bottle. Dealing with this man is utterly exhausting. I don't know why, but he's just not getting it. Meanwhile, I and everyone I know is in danger of being the next victim in the as of yet unknown murderer's killing spree.

"May I take the envelopes along with the letters? We can check for fingerprints and anything else that might indicate who the sender is."

I shrug, unsure what to do other than agree with him now. "Sure. Let me go get the envelope from the first one. The one from today's letter is on my coffee table."

As I trudge off toward my bedroom one more time, I wonder how anyone ever gets caught breaking the law if all the police in this town are like Officer Thompson. It's like the man hears what I'm saying but isn't actually listening.

I return to my living room to find him waiting for me. He's put the two letters and today's envelope into a gallon size plastic bag and holds it out for me to slip the first letter inside.

"My fingerprints are all over all of those," I say. "I didn't think to wear gloves when I got them."

Not that I have a spare pair of latex gloves lying around.

"I know," he says with a smile. "We'll take that into consideration."

With that, he starts walking toward the door. I guess that's it. Nice talk. Let's never do this again, Officer Thompson, okay?

Then I remember he never even asked to see the private messages on Instagram. "Um, don't you want to read what they sent me online?"

He stops and turns around to face me, his expression the definition of sheepishness. "Sorry, yes, I do."

I'm doomed. This man couldn't find his ass with both hands.

After bringing up the museum's account, I set my phone on the countertop in front of him. "That's them. Before you ask, no, I don't recognize the account that sent them. I looked and it said the account is private."

Officer Thompson doesn't say a word while he reads through both threatening messages. When he finishes, he looks at me and grimaces. "You seem to have made an enemy, Miss Mitchell."

Doomed. I honestly don't think he could find his ass with both hands and GPS.

"Yeah, thanks."

I watch as he writes down an email address on a piece of his little notebook paper and rips it out, setting it on the counter next to my phone. "Please send me a screenshot of both of those messages. I want to read through them again and compare the wording and language used to what was used in the letters."

I try to smile as I say, "Sure. I'll do it as soon as you leave."

"Thank you."

I follow him to the door, and when he steps out into the hallway, he turns around and says, "Keep your doors locked at all times. Avoid going out alone anytime but especially after dark. If you receive any more letters, please call me. Do you still have my card I gave you the other day? If not, I can write down my direct number for you too."

The other day when he questioned me for hours after

I found my boss hanging lifelessly among a sea of broken dolls.

Nodding, I answer, "I do."

He stares at me like he expects me to say something else, but there's nothing else to say. I have no idea if he's taking any of this seriously, or if it's all helping him confirm his belief that I had something to do with my boss's murder.

As I go to close the door without even saying goodbye, he stops it with his hand. Surprised, I wait for him to say something since it's clear he doesn't think we're done yet.

And when he finally does speak, I'm the happiest I've been in days.

"For the record, Miss Mitchell, I don't think you killed your boss. As you said the other day, you're too small to hoist him up in that noose."

I smile as relief washes over me. "Thank you. I didn't kill him, and all I want is for you to find who did so two crimes are solved."

Then he speaks again, and all the happiness I momentarily felt is wiped away.

"I do think, though, that whoever did wants me to think you're to blame. That's something we should both be concerned about."

As my heart sinks, I close the door behind him and lock it. I walk over to the couch and practically collapse onto it, so tired after all that's happened since the museum benefit.

In my head, I run down the last few days. My boss is dead after warning me about Nicholas, someone he supposedly thought of as a friend. I found him hanging in that scary doll storage room, which may be symbolic, but I don't know why. Now I'm receiving threatening letters some madman is hand-delivering to my home, which also let me know I've been receiving equally threatening messages online.

And then, as if fate wants me to know I missed something, my phone begins to vibrate with a text from Chase.

Fabulous.

16

As usual, my ex messages five times with all the same thought. He wants me back. We're made for each other. She didn't mean a thing to him. I'm the only girl he's ever loved.

Why does he keep sending these texts? He's been at it for days, and it hasn't worked even a single time. Why bother?

I wait for the inevitable phone call he always makes once he realizes I'm not going to answer any of his messages. Staring at my cell as it sits on the couch next to me, I silently will it to suddenly lose all its juice and turn off, saving me from having to hear it ring when he calls.

My attempt at mentally persuading my cell phone to do as I want fails miserably, and a minute later, his name pops up on my screen. I look at it flash once and then twice, all the while debating with myself whether or not I should answer it.

What's the point? It's not like I'm going to miss anything if I don't answer. He's only going to call again.

My phone stops its whining but only for a second before Chase's name flashes on my screen again. I have to give him credit. He's a terrible boyfriend and a crazy ex-boyfriend, but he's insistent, to say the least.

I grab it off the table and snap, "What? What do you want?"

My question is met with silence for a long moment before he says, "I heard about your boss."

Great. Now even my ex wants to talk about Mr. James.

"Oh yeah? Well, that's nice," I say in the least friendly tone I can muster as I sag back onto the couch cushion.

"How...how are you holding up?" Chase asks with concern in his voice, surprising me.

He's never been exactly a caring individual. Chase Kerrick thinks being nice is for other people.

I can't help but soften my attitude toward him when I realize he's attempting to be thoughtful for once. "It's been very hard, if I'm being honest. I found him, so there's that."

"Jesus, Carey. Thank God you aren't one of those women who get scared because that shit would give most people nightmares."

"I might not ever have nightmares, but that doesn't mean I want to find dead people."

My lame attempt to stand up for myself with him doesn't land the way I wanted, and he continues to talk about my boss and how young he was to hang himself. Clearly, Chase hasn't been told it wasn't a suicide.

I don't plan to enlighten him either. Let him go find Officer Thompson if he wants the details.

"Chase, did you call me just to talk about the death of

my boss? You never even met him, so I don't know why you'd care one way or the other about him."

In his typical style, he says, "I don't really, but I thought you might want someone to talk to."

"I'm good, but thanks."

Although I make sure that sounds like a definitive ending to our conversation, he ignores all the signs and continues to talk. "Then we can discuss us getting back together. I know you're missing me as much as I'm missing you, Carey."

"You cheated on me, Chase. I told you the day I found out, and I'll tell you again now. We have nothing to talk about."

"Don't say that. We do. I told you I'm never going to give up."

Suddenly, I have to wonder if it really is Chase sending me those threatening letters. "Oh? Does that mean you plan to stalk me until I give in? Or maybe you already have started stalking me."

"Stalking? What are you talking about, Carey? I know where you live and where you work. I know everything about you. I don't have to stalk you. I can just call you or show up where you're at."

Chase Kerrick has never been a bright man, but his answer tells me not only is he clueless but he's not the person behind those threatening letters either. He just doesn't have the intelligence necessary to do that. His style is blunt force. He would never be able to control himself long enough to threaten me through Instagram messages or letters. That would take too long, and the man simply doesn't have the patience.

"I have to go. Please don't call or text again. I won't be answering."

I say that knowing he won't listen or do as I ask. It's just not in his nature.

"You know I can't stop. I want you back, and until that happens, I'm going to keep showing you how much I care."

Hassling a person over the phone is caring now. Good to know. What kind of misguided soul thinks that?

"Goodbye, Chase."

After ending the call, I toss my phone toward the end of my couch and lie back, closing my eyes. Pinching the bridge of my nose, I try to forestall a headache, but it's no use. My skull feels like someone has put my head in a vice.

SOMEONE BANGING on my front door wakes me, and I scramble to get up off the couch to see who it is. Still groggy, I stumble across the room as I begin to wake up. This better not be Chase because if it is, I'm going to be so damn pissed. It would be just like him to graduate from simply harassing me over the phone and through texts to bothering me in person.

"Who is it?" I ask as I'm about to open the door, nearly forgetting what Officer Thompson told me just before he left.

"It's me!" Jenna says through the door.

Thank God. I don't think I could handle dealing with my ex in person today.

I open the door, and Jenna comes marching into my apartment, obviously flustered about something. She can get a bit emotional about work, so she's probably here to complain about one of her co-workers.

It'll be good to listen to someone else's problems for a while. Maybe it will take my mind off my own.

"What's up?" I ask as I close the door and head for the kitchen to grab a drink with caffeine to wake me up.

She stares at me like that question is odd. What's going on with her? Oh, God! Did that sous chef she's always complaining about finally do something to get her fired? She's been concerned about that for months, but I thought it was just her worrying needlessly since she's a great chef.

"What?" I ask as she plops down in the chair facing the kitchen so she can talk to me.

"I thought you'd be a little more torn up, but honestly, this is good. He was a jackass, Carey."

Either I'm still napping, or she's not making any sense. Whichever it is, I need a drink right now.

Grabbing a can of soda from the refrigerator, I gulp down half of it before walking into the living room to talk to Jenna. I'm mostly awake now, which means maybe I'll understand what the hell she's talking about.

I sit down on the couch where I'd been comfortably sleeping until a few minutes ago and run my hand through my hair. "Sorry, I was asleep. I guess I was tired, and I crashed a few hours ago."

Suddenly, I realize I don't know what time it is and turn to look at the window. It's dark out now. I must have slept for longer than I thought.

Jenna continues to look at me oddly, so I smooth my hair, sure I must look like a disaster. "I'm assuming you're wondering why I look like such a mess. I guess I must have tossed and turned a lot during my nap."

She draws her eyebrows in like she's angry, which only confuses me more. What is wrong with her?

"Did something happen at work?" Then I remember it's dark out. Why isn't she at work already?

"Jenna, what the hell is going on? Shouldn't you be at the restaurant?" I ask, sure something finally happened with her and that sous chef.

After letting out a huge sigh, she says, "You haven't heard, have you?"

I shake my head. "No. I told you. I was asleep. What's up?"

"Honey, they found Chase in his car this afternoon. He was dead."

The way she says that, like any of it could possibly be true, makes me sure I'm still sleeping. Okay, since this is clearly a dream, I guess I'll go along with her.

With a smile, I say, "Sure. If that's true, then why would you be the one to tell me? I can't imagine it's all over the news already."

Jenna frowns and sighs heavily again. "Carey, don't you remember? He and I live only a block away from one another. I saw the police cars come screaming into the parking lot right near his apartment about two hours ago, so I walked down to see what was up. A crowd had formed, so I asked one of the guys there, and he told me someone was found dead in his car. I looked and saw it was Chase's. I remembered he had the tinted windows on his black Corolla, and then I saw his license plate and knew it was him. L8RG8R, right?"

She spells out the way Chase thought was a clever way to say later gator on his license plate. I always thought it was stupid, but he thought he was just too smart when he got it last year after he bought his new car. I used to tell him I felt stupid riding around in a car with that idiotic plate.

I can't believe what Jenna's saying. She has to be mistaken. Chase can't be dead. I just talked to him before I fell asleep.

Shaking my head, I laugh at how absurd all this sounds. "There must be some mix-up. I just spoke to him a few hours ago. He's been calling me every day trying to get back together. The guy has a one-track mind."

My friend comes over to sit next to me and takes my hand in hers. Giving it a gentle squeeze, she says, "Carey, it's not a mistake. Chase is dead."

I study her face to see why she thinks this kind of joke is anywhere close to funny, but all I see is a look that tells me she's serious. This is impossible. Men in their late twenties don't just keel over dead one afternoon. He sounded perfectly fine when I spoke to him.

Everything in front of my eyes feels like it's spinning. This can't be happening. First Mr. James and now Chase. How could this be?

"How? I don't understand. How could this have happened?"

As soon as those words leave my lips, I break down. Sobbing into my hands, I think about how dismissive I was with him all the times he called and texted me. The man just wanted to get back together with me, and all I could do was tell him to go away.

I'm a monster.

"Oh, Carey," Jenna says as she wraps her arms around my shoulder. "It'll be okay."

I lift my head and stare at her through teary eyes. "How? How is it going to be okay? Chase is dead. I've had to deal with two people in my life dying in less than a month. I can't believe this is happening."

She nods like she understands, but how could she? How could anyone comprehend how it feels to lose two people in such a short time?

"I just meant you're going to be okay. That's it. You don't deserve to have this happen to you. You're so sweet, and I just don't know why this would be happening to you."

The way she says that sounds like I'm a selfish, terrible person. "It is happening to me, but two people are dead, Jenna. What's worse is I was warned about this."

She narrows her eyes and stares at me with a look of utter disbelief. "What do you mean? How could you know Chase would die?"

As I wipe my eyes, I explain the whole situation to her. "I started getting letters slipped under my door in the last few days. I told you about the first one, but I got another. The second one said someone else was going to die. I told that stupid cop, but he didn't take them seriously. Oh, God. Should I have mentioned it to everyone I know so they could be careful? Maybe Chase would be alive right now if I had."

Just the thought that I'm partly responsible because I

didn't tell him about the threat makes me sadder than I ever thought I could be. Why didn't I say anything? Why didn't I make a bigger deal about those damn letters to Officer Thompson? If I had, he may have been able to do something. It's not like I know hundreds of people. He would have had to talk to Chase, Emory, Jenna, and Nicholas. Oh, and my family, but they don't even live around here. God, what's happening?

Jenna gently rubs my back to ease my sadness. "I don't think that would have helped, to be honest. Anyway, how could you have known? You were just doing what you thought was right by telling Chase you didn't want to get back together. Remember, it was his fault you two broke up. If he hadn't cheated on you, there never would have been a reason for you to tell him you never wanted to see him again."

Hearing my own words, my own cruel and heartless words, makes me break down again. I told him I didn't want to see him again, and now he's dead. How could I have been so unkind to someone I said I loved?

In the midst of my misery, someone else knocks on my door. I turn to look at it with nothing but pure fear, dreading who may be on the other side.

I shake my head, unable to deal with anyone else now. "Can you answer it? I can't talk to anyone in the state I'm in."

"Sure. What if it's Emory?" Jenna asks as I stand to go to my room.

"Let her in, if it's her, but anyone else, I don't want to speak to them. Tell them to come back some other time."

"Okay. You go rest. I'll handle whoever it is, and then I can stay if you want me to. Just say the word."

"No, I'm fine alone. I just want to crawl into my bed, pull the covers over my head, and hide away until I feel better."

I hurry toward my room as I listen to hear who it is at my door. Jenna answers it, and instantly, I hear the voice of the only person I absolutely don't want to speak to right now.

"I'm looking for Carey Mitchell. Tell her it's Officer Thompson here to see her," he says in that smug tone I've hated since the first time I had to speak to him that day Emory and I found Mr. James hanging in the doll room.

I wait for Jenna to tell him what I said to say, and like the good friend she is, she says it word for word, making sure to put a little edge on each syllable so he knows his timing is terrible. I've just lost my ex-boyfriend, for God's sake. Is now really the best time to come bother me about questions regarding the death of my boss?

"Well, I really need to speak to her," Officer Thompson says with an edge of his own.

Thankfully, Jenna isn't having any of his attitude. "I'll tell her you came by. I suggest you call her first when you want to speak to her next time."

And with that, I hear my front door close and silently cheer on my dear friend. Imagine the nerve of that guy just stopping by like I'm here at his beck and call to harass yet again regarding his case.

Whatever he wants to ask me about Mr. James's death can wait. I've got more important things to deal with now.

Maybe if he hadn't been so blasé about those threatening letters I've been getting, Chase might still be alive.

Officer Thompson should be thanking his lucky stars I didn't answer the door.

I climb into bed, and a few seconds later, Jenna pokes her head into my room. With a big smile, she says, "I told that cop to call next time. He's a nervy one, isn't he? I thought at any moment he was just going to push me aside and barge right in. He's gone now, though. Are you sure you don't want me to stick around? I can. I don't have work tonight."

"No, but thank you. I just want to be alone right now."

"Okay, honey. I'll call you tomorrow to make sure everything's okay. Have a good night."

I watch as she disappears behind my bedroom door, and I pull the covers up over my head. I don't think I can handle much more. Two deaths in one person's life in a span of two weeks has to be strange.

Doesn't it?

17

I know the moment I hear the knocking who it is. I don't even have to get up and look out the peephole.

Staring at the door, I silently will Officer Thompson to go away. Not permanently. I wouldn't want to wish that on him. God forbid if he actually died after I did that. I might end up in a mental hospital.

No, I just want him to leave me alone for a few days. Is that so much to ask?

Then again, maybe he doesn't know Chase passed away. I want to think he doesn't and has a heart, but I'm not sure. Nothing in my experience with him says he's a caring person.

Just an officious one.

The knocking stops for a few brief seconds before it starts up again, and I know I can't avoid him any longer. It's been nearly twenty-four hours since he showed up and spoke to Jenna. I get the feeling he's going to continue pestering me if I don't answer the door and talk to him.

My feet feel like they're made of lead as I walk over to my door and look through the peephole, secretly hoping against hope that it won't be him. Unfortunately, it's him. He's wearing his dark blue police uniform, and I can see his nametag above his breast pocket.

Terrific.

Well, I might as well get this over with. I'm sure he only wants to go over what I said about finding Mr. James for the tenth time. Or maybe he wants to tell me he has a clue who's been sending me those messages and letters. That would be nice.

I take a deep breath in and let it out slowly, hoping to calm myself. Part of me wants to ream this guy out for being an insensitive jackass, while another part of me is just scared he's going to try to blame my boss's death on me this time. Both parts have the effect of making me a nervous wreck whenever Officer Thompson comes around.

Knowing I can't put this off forever, I steel myself for this meeting with him and slowly open the door. He stares directly into my eyes, which I assume is some cop trick he learned that's supposed to make my tongue looser.

All it makes me want to do is slam this door shut and never open it again.

"Miss Mitchell, I came by yesterday and spoke to a friend of yours who answered the door. Did she tell you I wanted to speak to you?"

I swear every word out of this man's mouth makes me want to scream.

"Yes, she did. I wasn't feeling well, so I told her I didn't want to speak to anyone yesterday."

Normally, I'd ask how I can help him or invite him in, but I'm not feeling in the mood to be pleasant today, and particularly not with Officer Thompson. I don't know what it is about him, but he grates on my very last nerve.

"I'd like to talk to you now. Do you have time?" he asks while he peeks over my shoulder like he's trying to see if I have anyone here with me.

I could lie. He'd never know I wasn't telling the absolute truth. I don't actually have time right now. I'm busy mourning Chase's death, not that I want to tell this guy about that. He'll have me indicted as a double murderer by breakfast time tomorrow.

Better to just get it over with so he can go and leave me alone.

I step back out of the way so he can come into my apartment as I say, "I can talk, but I'm not really feeling wonderful today, so if some of what I have to say sounds off, that's why."

Damn, that sounds incredibly suspicious. I better offer more explanation.

"Someone close to me passed away yesterday, and I'm pretty shaken up by it."

When I close the door and follow him to my kitchen, he says, "Yes, I know. That's actually why I'm here."

I stare at him utterly baffled about what he means. How could he know about Chase?

"You're not here to talk about my boss?"

He takes out his little notepad and pen from his pocket and shakes his head. "Not today. This visit is about

Chase Kerrick. He was your ex-boyfriend, right? The one who was harassing you?"

The way he says that makes Chase sound like a full-fledged stalker and not just some lovesick man who wanted to win me back. Why does Officer Thompson have to act like this?

"Yes, he was my ex. Chase wanted us to get back together, so he was calling and texting me hoping that would happen. Why are you asking about him?"

I expect him to jot down something, but instead, he simply stares into my eyes like he's trying to decipher if I'm telling him the truth. What the hell is this all about?

"Mr. Kerrick was murdered, just like Mr. James was."

My emotions begin to unravel inside me. He thinks I had something to do with the deaths of these men!

"Oh, so you naturally jump to the conclusion that because I knew two people who died that I must be involved, right?" I stop to take a breath and then spin around to grab a soda from my refrigerator. "Well, you're wrong. Yes, I knew both Mr. James and Chase, but the only connection between the three of us is I'm mourning their deaths. How dare you come here acting like I'm somehow to blame for anything that happened to either one of them?"

Even doing my best to channel Emory's strength, my hands still shake like I'm having some kind of nervous fit. Do the police routinely jump to erroneous conclusions, or is that just a specialty with this officer?

When Officer Thompson doesn't say anything in response to my outburst, I can't stop myself from adding one more comment. "And by the way, maybe if you hadn't dismissed those threatening letters, you could have alerted people in my life that they may be in danger. Chase may still be alive today, if you had."

For a split second, a look of hurt crosses the policeman's face, but it disappears as fast as it came. In its place, a serious expression settles into his features.

"Miss Mitchell, while I'm sorry for your loss, I do find it odd that you seem to be the one person who links these two deaths. You haven't asked how Chase died. Why? Is it that you know already?"

My hands shake so badly that I nearly drop the can of soda I'm holding. Did he just accuse me of killing my ex?

"I didn't ask because I'm not sure I can handle knowing right now. Have you ever lost someone you cared about, Officer Thompson? If so, you don't act like you remember how it feels. I don't need to know chapter and verse about how Chase died. It's enough to know my ex-boyfriend isn't alive anymore. That's upsetting enough. Trust me on that."

The truth is I don't want to know how Chase died. Be it suicide, accident, or murder, I don't care. All that matters is he's gone. For all the times I swore I hated him after I found out he cheated on me and all the times I said I never wanted to hear from him again, I never wanted him to die. I still loved him. I actually hoped that maybe one day we could be friends.

Even though I just told this officer I wasn't sure I wanted to know what happened, he blurts out, "He was strangled, just like your boss. I find that odd. Don't you?"

Tired of his ham-handed innuendos, I snap, "Don't I what? Find it odd that two grown men who are stronger than me and weigh more than I do by at least fifty pounds were strangled?"

For the first time, Officer Thompson looks embarrassed and drops his gaze to his notebook. "It doesn't take much to strangle someone, Miss Mitchell. It's actually far easier than most people think."

"Well, this person couldn't strangle anyone, and by the way, she wouldn't hurt a fly. Why you can't see that is beyond me. I didn't do anything to my boss or my ex. It's disappointing that the police in this town aren't actually running down leads instead of harassing someone who's in mourning for the second time in two weeks."

The words barely leave my mouth before I begin crying. I don't want to fall apart in front of this man since he's probably at this very moment thinking this is evidence of my guilt, but I can't help it. First, Mr. James is murdered, and now I find out Chase was murdered too? And both by strangulation?

For the first time, a terrible thought creeps into my brain. Is someone killing people around me to set me up to look like I had something to do with these deaths?

"Miss Mitchell? Are you okay?" my least favorite cop in the world asks, barely able to sound human and never reaching a point where he sounds like he cares even the slightest.

I let myself have a good old-fashioned sobfest right there in front of him, not caring in the least that he may feel uncomfortable while I let out my sadness. If he doesn't like it, he can leave. Nobody's keeping him here.

When I finally finish, I wipe my eyes and take a deep breath. I feel better, even if he doesn't.

"The answer to your question is no, I'm not okay. Two people I cared about are dead, and I've been getting threatening messages and letters, the last one practically predicting Chase would be killed. I know what you're thinking. You think I had something to do with both murders. Well, you're wrong. I didn't lie before when I said I couldn't hurt a fly. I don't care how little effort it takes to strangle someone, I couldn't do it. I don't know what to say to you to make you understand that, but there you go."

When I finish, he blows the air out of his mouth like this entire meeting has been far more emotional than he has the bandwidth to handle. I know how he feels. This has been a draining visit for me too.

"Do you have any ideas on who could have wanted either Mr. James or Mr. Kerrick dead?" he asks, and in his tone I hear frustration.

"No. For the thousandth time, I barely knew Mr. James other than he was my boss and I worked under him at the toy museum. I knew Chase, obviously, but I don't think anyone would want to kill him. Chase was a clown at times, which I'm sure infuriated some people on occasion, but that's not enough to kill him."

I stop talking for a moment and consider if I should admit there could be a connection between the two of them because of me. Officer Thompson doesn't need any more reasons to think I'm involved somehow, but it seems silly to ignore the obvious.

"As much as I don't want to admit it, I am likely the

only person both of those men had in common. Chase never met my boss, if that matters. He thought the toy museum was creepy and never visited there even once. And Mr. James never met my ex. I never took Chase to any of the events at the museum, again because he was creeped out by the things we have there."

The cop jots down notes as I speak and then looks up at me. "Did he really have a problem with the exhibits at the toy museum?"

Exhausted by his questions and my emotions churning inside me, I nod. "Yeah. Lots of people do. In fact, it was one of the main areas of focus for Mr. James. People don't get creeped out by Slinkies or See and Says, but dolls tend to scare people. You saw that room my boss was found in. Creepy. Even I can admit that. We do try to make sure the exhibits are far friendlier, though. The people who work on them try very hard, in fact."

"I can understand that."

We settle into an uneasy silence until he says, "Would it surprise you to find out Chase Kerrick was found with a doll's head in his car?"

I take a step back as his question filters through my brain. Shaking my head, I stammer out, "A wh-what?"

"A doll's head. We found it in the passenger seat. If I didn't know better, I'd say it's just like the ones in that room where Mr. James was found murdered."

None of what he's saying makes sense. Chase would never be driving around with a doll's head in his car. Nobody would. What the hell is going on?

"My ex thought those were the creepiest things at the

museum. He wouldn't have one of them anywhere near him. Trust me on this, Officer Thompson. Chase hated dolls."

The cop nods and writes in his notepad VICTIM WAS AFRAID OF DOLLS while I try to get a handle on the idea that the person who's sending me letters truly did carry out his threat. Then a terrible thought pops into my mind.

Is it someone from the museum killing people? Clearly, that's what the police think, but they've decided it's me since I knew both the victims.

I need to show Officer Thompson he's wrong, or he's never going to find the real killer.

Hoping he'll understand I'm innocent, I say, "I know you're intent on drawing a straight line between me and the victims, but have you checked out everyone else who works at the museum? Mr. James being found in the doll storage room is strange enough, but you finding a doll's head in Chase's car is simply bizarre. My boss definitely would go to that storage room if he needed something, but I know with all my heart that Chase Kerrick would never keep a doll's head anywhere near him. Someone is trying to make it seem like I'm the person responsible for both these murders, but I didn't do anything."

Officer Thompson closes his notebook and stuffs it back into his shirt pocket along with the pen. "That scenario is possible, but put yourself in my shoes, Miss Mitchell. You knew both victims. You had problems with both victims. Both victims were found around doll heads. It sort of jumps off the page, don't you think?"

I stopped listening when he said I had problems with both Mr. James and Chase. I swear this cop is either the worst at what he does or just has it out for me. Why distort the facts like that?

"First of all, I didn't have any problems with my boss. He was a boss, which meant he could be difficult sometimes. I'm sure you can say the same thing about your boss. To say that I had a problem with Mr. James is wrong. And second of all, I didn't have a problem with Chase. Yes, he was bothering me with his calls and texts because they kept reminding me that he cheated on me and broke my heart. Yes, I broke up with him. But none of that meant I had a problem with him. I loved Chase. I had hoped we could be friends once this awkward post-breakup phase was over. So please stop trying to make it seem like I had an ax to grind with either of them because I didn't."

Before Officer Thompson has a chance to think up other ways I'm guilty, I say to him, "Now if you will please leave, I want to be alone. Regardless of what you think, I'm mourning the death of someone I truly cared about."

He doesn't say a word but simply nods before turning to walk toward the door, surprising me. I feared he'd try to stick around to ask me more questions I don't have the answers to or to once more insinuate I'm the only person who could have killed both my boss and my ex-boyfriend.

When he steps out into the hallway, he stops and says, "We haven't found out anything definitive about those letters yet. I'm assuming you haven't received any more?"

"You really do think the worst of me, don't you? If I get any more, as much as I'm beginning to hate these little get-togethers with you, I'll let you know. Maybe you could try not being so damn sure it's me who's killing people and try looking for the actual killer instead."

I don't give him a chance to respond before I calmly shut the door and lock it.

18

WHAT DID you think about the doll's head in your boyfriend's car? Did you think it was a nice touch?

So you and that cop seem to be spending a lot of time together. Is this a new relationship? Or is he thinking you're the reason both those men are dead?

You know he believes you're the one responsible, right? It's logical. Those men had nothing in common. One was middle aged and worked at a toy museum. He devoted every waking minute to that place. Nothing mattered more to your boss. Then again, you know that. You did work closely with him, after all.

The other was a man who hadn't even reached thirty. He hated that museum because it gave him the creeps. How many times did he say that to you? It actually got to the point that you didn't even talk about work anymore because he hated that toy museum so much.

So it makes sense that good old Officer Thompson is working from the belief that you're the connection between the victims. He's a bit slow on the uptake, but what do you expect when they both knew you?

The doll's head in your ex's car felt like a bit much, but if you're going to do something, you should do it right. See, the authorities need to focus on you, so it had to be an item that made it seem like it came from that museum of yours.

Are you feeling stressed out with how often Officer Thompson has been visiting you about all of this? Knowing you, you're practically falling apart.

Oh, yes. I know all about you.

So now the cops are really paying attention to you. That definitely isn't something you like. That's for sure. They're finding out things about you that may seem innocent enough, but considering two men are dead and the only connection between them is you, they can't help but wonder.

How's it feel being looked at like you're a murderer? Soon people on the street will begin to murmur when you walk by. Maybe someone at the museum will hear the police are looking at you in this investigation.

Just wait until the next person dies.

It's almost time to become public enemy number one, Carey. Are you ready?

19

MY HAND SHAKES as I reread the latest letter slipped under my door. All I can wonder is why whoever this is wants to do this to me. Why are they targeting me, of all people? Is this revenge for something I've done?

But what? I barely have a social life. I work and come home most days. Who could I have upset so much that they want to frame me for Mr. James's and Chase's murders?

I throw the letter on my coffee table before collapsing onto my couch. I can't think of who could be behind this. I'm not a bad person who treats people terribly. I always smile when I see my neighbors. Well, not those people with the teenagers who run wild, but nobody smiles at them. Everyone else, though, I'm nice to in my apartment complex.

No matter how hard I try, I can't come up with who's doing this. I need to, though, because they plan on continuing the killing.

I know I should just hand the letter over to Officer

Thompson, but I dread talking to him again. He says he doesn't think I'm to blame, but is he focusing on anyone else? It doesn't seem like he is.

Not wanting to deal with him directly, I take a picture of the letter and send it to his email like I did with the two private messages from Instagram. Now he can see it without bothering me.

As I try to get my focus on anything other than what my life has turned into, I close my eyes and do that technique that yoga lady taught Emory and me when my friend was in her yoga phase. That didn't last more than a few weeks, but I have to admit a lot of what that lady showed us is helpful.

Deep breaths in and then let them out slowly. Find a happy thought and focus your mind on that.

I push out all the bad and think about that time Emory, Jenna, and I spent a weekend at the beach. So often our schedules haven't synced up, but it happened a couple years ago, and the three of us reserved a room at a hotel just a block from the shore. That was before Jenna got engaged to that terrible guy who ended up stealing her entire life savings.

She was so happy that weekend. So was Emory. We spent hours on the sand and swimming in the ocean before heading back to the room and bingeing on junk food and margaritas.

Before Emory decided her body was a temple only deserving healthy food.

After a few minutes of remembering that weekend, I let out a heavy sigh of relief. I'm going to be okay. The police are going to figure out who's behind these threatening messages and letters, and no one else is going to be hurt.

There is no other choice but to believe that, or I'll never want to leave my apartment again.

I finally get to return to work on Monday, and although I've been complaining that I need a vacation for the past two years, this week has been the worst. I just want things to go back to normal as much as possible.

It's not too much to ask, is it?

Oh, God. I have to get through the memorial service for Mr. James this afternoon. I hear Chase's funeral will be on Wednesday, so I'll have to go to that too.

I used to think it was odd when my father got into his sixties and suddenly there was a funeral or memorial service he had to attend every other week. My mother used to joke that he needed to buy more suits because all his friends were suddenly dying.

That seems to be my life now, but it's thirty years too early. Thank God I like wearing black and have more than the one dress for a week that will involve two reasons to wear that color.

After taking a shower and doing my hair and makeup for the first time in two days, I stand in front of my full-length mirror and study my reflection in my new dress. All I can think is I look like my father today. Every time he had to go to a funeral for one of his friends, he wore the same expression I do right now.

A combination of miserable and confused with a dash of terrified thrown in.

My father worried he might be next with every time he had to say goodbye to one of his old buddies. My fear is because of something else, something just as terrifying as death.

I force a smile, but that does little to hide what I'm feeling. All I want is for all of this to end. No more people I care about dying. No more threatening letters. I just wish to go back to my boring life. I swear I'll never say I hate it and want something different and exciting to happen ever again.

Taking a deep breath in, I blow the air out of my lungs. "You can do this."

That I'm not sure I can is the real problem. Today, I have to be around all the people I've worked with for the past few years, and all I can think of is they see me like Officer Thompson does. In the entire time I've worked at the toy museum, I've never been unkind or rude once to anyone there. Doesn't that count for something?

Not when people think you're a murderer, Carey.

"No! I can't think like that. Today is about Mr. James and saying goodbye to the one person who did more for the museum than anyone else ever has. Nobody is even going to be thinking about you today, so enough with all the murderer nonsense. They know you."

I say all of this to my reflection, but she doesn't seem convinced either. Thankfully, someone knocking on my door tears me out of my doubt spiral, so I turn away from the look in her eyes that says what I fear is exactly what's going to happen.

My hands start to shake just before I reach my front door, but I silently will my fear to go away for the moment. Nicholas said he'd pick me up at two, and it's five minutes before, so I don't have to worry.

Throwing open the door, I see him standing there smiling wearing a black suit with a gray dress shirt and a black tie. Relief washes over me, although I know it was stupid to get worked up about just opening a door. The problem is between the visits from my least favorite cop in the world and those notes that have begun to appear, my front door has quickly become a nerve-wracking part of my home for me.

"Hi," he says, almost warily. "You look like you're surprised to see me."

I step back and wave him into my apartment. "No, not at all. Just happy to see you."

He stops just a few feet into my living room as I close the door and leans in to kiss me when I turn to face him. "I'm glad we can be there for each other today."

I smile and nod, still not understanding why Mr. James warned me against Nicholas. He's been nothing but a gentleman the entire time we've known one another. Every time we have a date, he's respectful and polite. What could possibly be wrong with him that made my boss think he should seek me out that night and warn me about being with him?

"Give me a couple minutes, okay? I just want to check my makeup and hair one last time before we leave."

He stares at me for a moment and smiles. "You look great, but take your time. I'll just be relaxing out here."

I hurry into my bedroom and check myself out one last time. I don't look too worse for wear, even though I've had the week from hell. I grab my powder brush and drag it over my face one last time before deciding this is as good as it gets.

When I return to the living room, Nicholas is sitting on my sofa grimacing like he's in pain. "Did you sit on a hair clip?" I ask, pretty sure I didn't leave one lying around.

He quickly stands up, shaking his head. "No. It's this suit."

"Don't you wear a suit to work every day?" I ask, not understanding what he means.

Nodding, he says, "I do, but I only wear this one for funerals. It's never felt right from the first time I put it on. I should have just had it altered, but instead I use it for occasions like this today."

"If it's any consolation, you look great. It suits you."

A slow smile lifts the corners of his mouth. "Did you just make a pun?"

For a second, I don't know what he means, but then I realize what I just said and laugh. "Unintentionally, yes."

"Let's keep that happy thought going all afternoon. Randall would have wanted it that way."

I don't ask why he thinks that, but the last thing I ever imagine when I think of my former boss is him wanting to see anyone happy. In all the time I worked with him, the man rarely cracked a smile or let out a chuckle. In fact, I'd say Mr. James was one of the most serious people I've ever encountered.

Then again, I wasn't close to him. I know Nicholas has said more than once he and my boss weren't actually friends, but more and more I have the sense that he must have known him better than I did. For God's sake, I never even knew Mr. James had a wife or that she died while I worked at the museum.

As Nicholas and I make our way down to his car, he weaves his fingers through mine and says, "What do you think after the memorial service we come back here and order some food to be delivered? We can just hunker down with one another to chase away the sadness I'm sure is going to be all of what today has for us."

Sure that's the sweetest idea anyone has ever suggested to me, I smile and give his hand a squeeze. "Okay. That's sounds good. I'm not sure I'm going to want to be alone after the service."

"Good," he says as he aims his key fob at his black BMW. "And by the way, how long we stay at this thing is entirely up to you. When you've had enough, just say the word and we're out of there."

I smile and nod, but I can't mistake how that last sentence he uttered was nowhere as sweet as his idea for what we should do after the service. Then again, everyone deals with their grief in their own way. Perhaps Nicholas is a man who doesn't prefer these public displays of sadness.

AFTER A MEMORIAL SERVICE that ran nearly an hour and included more than a dozen people talking about how wonderful Mr. James was at his job as the director of the toy museum, Nicholas and I stand off to the side in the same room where we met just a couple weeks ago. As I watch people mingle, I can't help but think this day is much like that one at the benefit.

Except Mr. James isn't here to see it.

"I think my boss would have been touched to see how many people have come today," I say quietly to Nicholas.

He scans the crowded room and nods. "He always loved when he could get people to come to this place. It was his life's mission to make the museum bigger than when he started here."

I smile as I remember Mr. James always saying how much he hoped he could get the museum to be more popular with schoolteachers. He was convinced that would make what we do here more popular. So he made sure to reach out to local schools whenever we had a new exhibit go up, and he never failed to spend each August and September telling any school administrator who would listen that the toy museum was a great place for students to learn.

He had to persuade more than a few that this wasn't merely a spot for playing, which he believed was important too, but it was a place where children could learn why toys were so important to all ages. I used to dread the end of the summer each year because he'd become even more difficult to work with when he had to constantly struggle to show people the worth of the museum. I never realized until this moment how hard that must have been for him.

As I remember that, Misha walks toward us with a tissue in her hand she uses to dab under her eyes. She stops in front of us and sighs before putting on her best smile.

"He would have been so happy to see all these people turn out today. Mr. James never cared why people came here. He just cared that they came because once they saw what we have to offer, he was sure they'd tell people and they'd come back again and again," she says, nearly sobbing by the time she finishes.

I reach out to hug her, and she wraps her arms around me as she begins to cry in earnest. "I promised myself I wouldn't let the tears start, and here I am crying like a baby. You're so strong, Carey. I wish I was like you."

As I hold her and gently pat her back, I can't help but feel like a fraud. It's not strength that's keeping me from crying. It's pure, unadulterated fear. Misha has no idea what's been going on with me since we last talked. The threatening letters. Dealing with Officer Thompson. The death of a second person I know. All of it has left me with no emotions but fear.

"It's okay, Misha. I know how you feel."

She stands there hugging me tightly for another minute or so sobbing as I smell her perfume and can't help but be reminded of my mother because she used to wear something similar. The fragrance is flowery with a hint of earthy undertones. It's a soft scent I always associated with my parents going out somewhere special because that's the only time she ever wore perfume.

When Misha steps back away from me, she wipes under her eyes with that tissue that's ratty after so much use. "I thought you might say a few words today, but I understand why you chose not to."

I smile and fake sniffle, as if I'm as upset as she is. "I just wasn't sure I could get through standing up in front of everyone without falling apart, and no one wants to see me do that, right?"

Misha gently touches my arm and nods her head. "I

completely understand. I wouldn't have been able to do it. Look at me. I can barely talk to someone without becoming a mess. Can you imagine what I would have been like up there at the front of the room?"

Turning my head, I look at Nicholas and see him nodding too. Neither of them have any idea of the real reason why I chose not to speak at Mr. James's memorial service. They think it's because I'd be like Misha.

The truth is since my boss died I've realized I barely knew him at all. What right do I have to stand up in front of all of these people and say some nice words about someone who was practically a stranger to me?

Feeling like I need to say something, I touch Misha's hand and say, "He knew how we all felt about him."

Not exactly the most heartfelt sentiment anyone has ever uttered, but she takes it in the spirit it was meant and smiles. "He did. It's just not going to be the same around here without him. Well, I better go. I'll see you on Monday?"

"I'll be here," I say, trying to sound upbeat but instantly dreading the thought that by that time someone will have heard about Chase's death.

When she walks away, Nicholas nudges my arm. I turn to look at him, and he says, "You sound like you don't want to go back to work quite yet."

I can't tell him the real reason I'm uneasy about returning to my job, so I shrug. "It's just going to be different without Mr. James. I'm not sure what's going to happen or when they're going to hire someone new to replace him. Or maybe they won't and Michael will move into the position. Everything is really in flux right now, and that can be awkward in the workplace."

All of that is a lie, but I don't want Nicholas to know a second man in my life has died recently under similar circumstances to my boss's murder. It's not exactly the best thing for a new relationship.

"Want to go?" he asks after my big explanation.

"Sure. Just let me visit the ladies' room and then I'll be ready. Be right back."

I make my way through the crowd and head to the bathroom, happy no one stopped me to chat about how I'm doing. The last thing I want to talk about are my feelings today. Not because I can't control my emotions but because I'm struggling to make it look like I have any about the last hour.

One of my co-workers follows me into the ladies' room, but thankfully, Monica doesn't attempt to strike up a conversation. By the time I get done and I'm standing in front of the mirror checking my makeup, she comes out of the stall, and I can tell she wants to talk.

Damn! Why didn't I just wash my hands and leave?

"How are you holding up?" she asks as she turns on the water.

"I'm okay. It's been rough, but I'm feeling okay now. How are you?" I ask, eager to take the focus off me and put it on her and her feelings.

As she finishes washing her hands and reaches for a paper towel, she sighs. "It's been such a shock. I bet it's been worse for you, though."

I nod, giving her a half-hearted smile. Everyone at the

museum thinks Mr. James and I must have been close. They have no idea how wrong that assumption is.

"It'll be strange working for someone else, but Michael's a wonderful person. I'm sure he's going to do well in the position."

Monica tosses the used paper towel into the wastebasket and shakes her head. "No, I mean because your ex died too this week."

Her words hit me like a slap to the face. Oh God! People know about Chase's death. They're all going to think I'm some kind of black widow.

My heart races, and my mouth instantly turns bone dry as I try to think of something to say. Sure she can see how upset I am, I nod and mumble, "Yes, it's been hard. Thanks."

Desperate to escape this conversation, I hurry out of the ladies' room and make a beeline for Nicholas still standing where I left him. I need to get him out of here before Monica or someone else brings up Chase's death.

"Okay, let's go," I say, my eyes scanning the room for any sign that my other co-workers already know.

He doesn't question why I seem to be in a hurry now and takes my hand as he walks with me toward the door. I don't care if it seems rude that we aren't saying goodbye to anyone. I can't take the chance someone will want to talk about how I'm the woman who personally knows two people who've been murdered in exactly the same way.

How am I going to return to work now?

20

THE SUN STREAMING through my bedroom window wakes me up, and I roll over to shield my eyes, nearly bumping into Nicholas, who's still asleep. After the memorial service, we came back here and hung out just like he suggested, ordering in Chinese food for dinner. One thing led to another, and here I am watching his chest rise and fall as he breathes in and out, a little surprised we slept together since it usually takes me longer before I know someone well enough to have sex with them but happy we got together.

"Are you watching me sleep?" he asks, his eyes still closed.

A little embarrassed he caught me, I joke, "No. If you're talking, then you're awake, so I'm technically not watching you sleep."

He opens his left eye and looks up at me, smiling. "I had no idea you'd be this cute in the morning."

Instantly, I slide my hands over my hair and hope it

doesn't look like a tangled mess. "Well, thank you. Cute is a nice thing to hear first thing in the morning."

I lean down and kiss him with my lips closed, desperate to avoid him smelling my morning breath that's probably ten times as bad as usual since I didn't brush my teeth after we slept together. He doesn't seem to have that hang up about his own breath and tries to slip his tongue over my lips, but I pull away, making sure to smile as I roll over to get out of bed.

"Do you drink coffee when you get up?" I ask as I search the floor for a T-shirt or something to throw on so I'm not walking around naked in the bright light of day.

I look back at him and see he's got his arms behind his head watching me as I frantically look for a way to cover up while he clearly feels more comfortable letting things all hang out. Literally. My eyes trail down his naked chest to where a moment ago the sheets were covering his bottom half, but he's pushed them off to reveal his entire body.

Obviously, he's more secure about his looks first thing in the morning than I am. Then again, if I had his muscular body, I probably would want to lie around buck naked all day too.

"Looking for something?" he asks with a chuckle just before I locate a T-shirt I only wore for a couple hours yesterday.

I quickly slip it over my head and wonder if I should bother to search for my underwear, not knowing where we tossed them last night in the heat of passion. Why I'm so insecure about my body I have no idea, but I've always been like this. I wish I was someone who could prance around nude and be comfortable. I really do.

But I'm not, and this morning isn't going to change that.

Flustered knowing he's watching me, I turn back to face him and smile. "I don't know if you answered about the coffee, but I sure could use some. Do you want a cup?"

"Definitely," he says with a wicked smile that reminds me of how he looked at me in that incredibly sexy way last night right before we came here to my bedroom.

"Okay, I'll go get that started. Be right back."

He stares at me as I hurry out of the room, and I wonder if I should have just stayed in bed. Maybe he assumed we'd have another round of sex this morning.

Not that I didn't want that. Who wouldn't want to enjoy sex with a gorgeous man who's great in bed? I just didn't know if that was on his mind, and then before I knew it, all I wanted to do was find something to wear so I wasn't completely naked.

As I stand at the kitchen counter scooping coffee into the filter, I remember how Chase used to reprimand me all the time about not being confident regarding my body. He'd say, "Carey, you look great. Why do you always think less of yourself than you should?"

And then he slept with another woman, so there's that.

I push that into the dark recesses of my mind where everything about Chase belongs and get the coffee maker doing its job. I don't know whether to go back into the bedroom or not, so I stand there listening to the appliance puffing and gurgling as I try to fully wake up.

That's a mistake, though, because as soon as I'm fully cognizant of what's going on, I remember what Monica said. Did she mention Chase's passing to anyone else? Or did someone mention it to her? Dear God. How many people at the museum know that two people in my life have died in the past two weeks?

I immediately correct myself. Not just died. Were murdered. In the same exact way. And with dolls around them. Well, only one doll head with Chase, but what does it matter? Anyone who hears about the similarities is going to wonder since the only thing Mr. James and my ex had in common was me.

Dread fills my brain as the coffee maker completes its task. Still staring at it, I don't notice the coffee's ready until Nicholas appears next to me and says something about it.

"Mind if I slide in there and grab a cup?"

I snap out of my panic fog about what everyone at the museum knows about me and my connection to two dead men and force a smile as I notice he's fully dressed in his suit and tie already. "Sure. Sorry. I guess I wasn't as awake as I should be to run machinery."

My attempt at humor makes Nicholas laugh, and as he reaches around me to start opening cabinets to find a cup, he presses a soft kiss to my cheek. "You're very cute in the morning. I like that."

His compliment eases my worry for the moment, and I say, "It's the cabinet to the right of you. Grab me one too."

Nodding, he gets two mugs off the bottom shelf and sets them down next to the coffee maker. I look and see he chose the Life's A Beach mug Emory bought me when she went to Myrtle Beach a couple summers ago and the mug I bought with two pink flamingos on each side that says Be a flamingo in a flock of pigeons during my attempt to be more confident last fall.

Nicholas studies them both for a long moment, and then turns his head to look at me. "Did you buy these? They're cute."

The first time he said I was cute was great. The second time I liked it because I had told a joke that went over well. Something about this mention of my being cute makes me think he doesn't like these mugs at all and thinks they're stupid.

I wave off the idea the mugs mean anything to me. "Gifts from friends. You know how it is. Someone goes on vacation, and they bring you back stuff you probably wouldn't normally buy for yourself. Do you take milk and sugar? I don't have any cream, unfortunately."

Before I can see if he believes my lie about the mug, I turn away from him and hurry over to the refrigerator to grab the carton of milk off the door. I haven't been to the grocery store in a while, so I hope the milk is still good and I have enough for both of us. At least I know I have a bowl full of sugar.

"No, I prefer black."

I don't say what I always tell Jenna when she orders her coffee that way. Gross. I can't imagine drinking coffee without something to take the bitterness out. I've tried every brand of coffee there is from the most expensive to the cheapest, and they all taste bitter without milk and sugar.

Oh well. At least if the milk has gone bad Nicholas won't have to miss out on his morning pick-me-up.

Shaking the milk carton, I judge I have just enough to make my coffee drinkable this morning. I point at the cabinet next to him and ask, "Can you grab the sugar bowl? It's on the second shelf."

He sets my white Martha Stewart sugar bowl down on the counter next to the mugs and grabs the flamingo one for himself. I watch him pour half a cup and then back away to let me in to get mine. Curious why he only took half a mugful, I pour mine and then turn around to ask him about it.

"Why only halfway?" I ask, pointing at the mug as he lifts it to his lips.

He takes a sip and then sets the mug down on the counter next to him. "It's more than enough caffeine for me. If I drink a whole cup, I'll be wired all day. Strange, huh?"

"No, not at all," I answer, sure I've never met any man who drank only half a cup of coffee a day. "I bet if you wanted to quit, you'd have no problem. Me? I'm a caffeine junkie in the morning. At least two cups before I go to work."

As soon as the word work comes out of my mouth, I feel my expression fall. Just thinking about going back now after talking to Monica yesterday makes me feel queasy. I want to believe I'm overreacting, but with the way life has been lately, I wouldn't be surprised if I walked into the museum on Monday and people threw stones at me.

"Something wrong, Carey?" Nicholas asks. "It's going back to work, isn't it?"

I nod, but the last thing I want to do is get into a conversation about the real reason why I'm dreading returning to work. I'd rather he merely think my grief over my boss's untimely death weighs heavily on me.

"It's just hard. You know how it is. You get used to your life being one way, and then one day, it's completely upended. I don't know what's going to happen with my new boss since he has an assistant already. Misha, the lady from yesterday who was having such a hard time."

My explanation seems to satisfy him, and he lifts his coffee mug up to his lips to take another sip. "Well, my offer still stands. You could come work for me."

"Thank you, but how would that work since we just slept together?" I ask with a chuckle.

He takes another drink and then tosses the rest of his coffee into the sink. "We'd have to not sleep together then. I better get going. I've got a ton of work to do."

His abrupt decision to leave throws me off a little, so I don't know what to say. I was only joking about the whole sleeping together thing. I understand if I ever did go to work for his company that we would have to be completely professional.

"Oh, okay."

I don't know what to say now. I think we're dating, especially after last night, but something in the way he seems so aloof at this moment makes me feel strange telling him to call me or asking when we're going to see each other again.

He leans in and kisses me on the cheek. "I'll give you a call."

I watch him walk out the door without saying another word to him. He'll give me a call? Why does that sound like something you say when you don't plan on ever seeing that person again but don't want to be an utter jackass after having sex with them?

Alone in my kitchen, I feel very much unlike those independent and beautiful flamingos on the mug he used. I don't even feel good enough to rank with the pigeons right now. I don't know what ranks below those trash birds, but whatever it is, that's what I feel like.

TWO DAYS. That's how long I've waited for Nicholas to call. Nearly forty-eight hours. It's been that long since we stood in my kitchen talking about silly mugs and how he drinks coffee before he said he'd call and unceremoniously walked out of my apartment after sleeping with me.

I stare at whatever show is on the television as I try to convince myself I'm being stupid about this. Nicholas and I don't talk every day. We don't even talk every two days, so all that time isn't that long for him to not call.

Except we slept together, so I thought he would call before now.

Lifting my glass, I take a drink of soda as I tell myself it's fine. So he hasn't called. Big deal. But then I hear my boss's voice echoing in my head warning me about Nicholas.

Is that what Mr. James meant? That Nicholas sleeps with women and then never calls them again?

Jesus, I don't need this now. Between the two deaths, those horrible, threatening letters, that infernal cop always showing up to talk about the cases, and worrying about what's going to happen when I go into work tomorrow morning, the last thing I want to deal with is raging insecurity after sleeping with a man because he hasn't called.

Reaching over to grab my phone off the coffee table, I look to see if I have any missed calls or messages from him. None. Zero. In fact, I have not a single call or text from anyone in the past two days.

Nice to know all the people in my life are concerned about me after two people have been murdered and I've been getting scared to death by those damn letters.

Needing to take my mind off everything before I spin out of control, I call Emory and hope I'm not interrupting her creating some masterpiece because her muse is finally working with her instead of against her. She answers quickly, which could mean she's feeling triumphant or completely lost and unable to create anything.

"Please tell me good news because if you don't, I might kill myself."

I don't say anything to that for a few seconds but then answer, "Uh, sorry, no can do. But please don't off yourself. I can't deal with anymore death right now."

"Oh, Carey. I'm so sorry. That was incredibly insensitive of me. Jesus, I'm such a moron. How could I say that?"

After refilling my glass, I walk into my living room and collapse onto the couch. "It's okay. I know you didn't mean anything by it. The muse not working with you today?"

"She's not working with me any day lately, it seems!" Emory yells, like she's addressing someone standing in the room with her.

"I'm sorry. And here I am calling to complain."

I hear noises in the background like she's moving furniture before she says, "It's okay. I'm all ears. Anything to take my mind off the barren wasteland that is my creative life at the moment."

She really is quite dramatic. I know she's an artist and they can be emotional at times, especially about their work, but it hasn't been that long that she's been unable to create anything. I'd tell her that, but I made that mistake once and won't do that again. The only thing worse than her being unhappy with her muse is her being unhappy with me.

Feeling like I should start my complaining off with a bang, I say, "I slept with Nicholas."

A deafening silence fills my ears, but I don't say anything since I'm guessing Emory needs a few moments to process that news. A free spirit, it's nothing for her to sleep with someone the first time she meets them. She says she can tell from just a few short minutes with a guy if she wants to have sex with him or not. I tend to take much longer, so my news about sleeping with Nicholas after only a couple weeks of knowing him definitely might be taking her aback.

Finally, she says, "Damn, Carey. Look at you! When did Carey Mitchell turn into a twenty-first century woman?"

"Ha-ha. Funny."

"So? Was he good? He's hot, so there's that. But did he have any skills in the sack?"

Nobody would ever accuse Emory of being a romantic. It's strange because she has all the trademarks of someone who would be into the emotional side of sex.

I try to think of a way to describe my time with Nicholas. It was very good, but if I tell her that, she'll want more details, and I really don't want to get into that conversation.

"In my opinion, it was damn good. Then again, I don't have the experience others have, so who knows?"

That last part was more deflection than anything else. Hopefully, she'll take the bait.

"It is true you've only had a few guys you've slept with, but if you enjoyed it, that's all that matters. Just tell me this. Does he look as good out of that expensive suit as he does in it?"

After a few seconds of hesitation, I smile and say, "Yes."

That's all she needs to go off on how hot men look wearing suits, and it's always great to see they have the goods underneath their clothes. I'll say this about Emory. She does have a genuine appreciation for men.

When she takes a break in her lecture on how suits

are the male equivalent of lingerie for women, I quietly say, "It's been two days, and he hasn't called."

"Hmmm...what's that about?"

That's what I'd like to know.

"I'm not sure. Two days isn't long, is it?" I ask, seeking some confirmation that he didn't just use me for sex.

That gets me a second hmmm and silence. Oh, God. It is a long time after someone has sex with you. I knew it!

"Do you think this is why your boss warned you about him?" Emory asks, surprising me for a moment.

"What? Oh, yeah. He did warn me about Nicholas, but I can't imagine that had anything to do with sex. My boss and I never talked about that topic. Ever."

"Well, maybe that's why he didn't say much. If he is a love 'em and leave 'em kind of guy, he's an ass. Don't get down about it."

That's easy for her to say. Emory would just go find another guy to sleep with and forget Nicholas. I'm not that way. Damnit, why did I go against everything I am and jump into bed with him so soon?

"I'd say it's too late for that," I say, sounding pathetic.

"You could call him. It is the twenty-first century, you know, and even though you're new to this time, it's a pretty common thing to do. Call him and see what's up," she says with enthusiasm.

I'd rather just sit here hating myself than take the chance of calling him and knowing he didn't care and just used me for sex. At least without hearing him say that I can live in the fantasy that everything's fine.

If only I could find a way to do that.

"Yeah, I'm not calling Nicholas. It would look desperate."

"It's not desperate to be confident and want to know what's going on, Carey. Call him and see what he says. At least you'd know one way or the other."

People always say that like knowing the truth in all situations is a good thing. It's not. I'd rather not know and live in a world where he might simply be busy. At least then I wouldn't feel completely used and thrown away.

Emory can't understand that, though. It's just not her style. I should have called Jenna. She'd get it.

"I better get going. I have to get ready for work tomorrow. It's my first day back, and I'm dreading it."

"Oh, okay. Don't sweat this whole Nicholas thing, honey. Whatever's meant to be will be."

My friend is never more insufferable than when she gets all philosophical. No one is. It never comes off as anything more than flippant, but if you try to tell anyone who spouts such nonsense that, they immediately say you're being touchy.

"Thanks. Good luck with the muse. I hope she gets back in line. I'll talk to you later."

The mere mention of her muse makes Emory groan, just as I knew it would. That was cruel and passive aggressive of me. I shouldn't have said anything.

"Call Jenna. She's better to talk to about men anyway, even though she usually hates them," Emory suggests. "Let me know what happens, okay? I'll be rooting for you."

I thank her as a rotten feeling fills me. Here she is on

my side, and I rub her nose in the fact that her muse isn't cooperating.

Maybe I deserve all the bad things happening to me.

21

IT'S NEARLY MID-AFTERNOON, but I call Jenna because I need to hear someone say something about this Nicholas situation that doesn't make me feel worse than I did when I woke up this morning after two days of hearing not a peep from him. Emory isn't exactly the sympathetic ear I need right now.

After three rings, I think about pressing END, but Jenna answers and doesn't even sound groggy. "Hey, you! What's up?"

Her chirper tone surprises me, but I say, "Not much. Just wanted to talk."

"Is that cop still hassling you? Or did the police actually do something right and find out who's sending you those letters?"

Leave it to Jenna to cut to the chase about that situation.

"He's let up a little in the past couple days, thankfully. As for the threatening letters and messages, they've stopped for the moment too, but the police haven't found who's behind them. Or if they have, they aren't telling me."

"Protect and serve my ass," she says, practically hissing out the words.

I don't say anything, wondering if I should even bother mentioning my issue with Nicholas not calling. Maybe it's nothing. Maybe Emory is right about me being too old-fashioned. It's just sex, right? I shouldn't make such a big deal out of it.

When I don't continue the conversation, Jenna asks, "What's wrong? You're not talking. Is something going on? Is this about Chase?"

She sounds genuinely worried, so I answer, "I think I have a problem. Or maybe I don't. I don't know."

"I'm intrigued. What problem?"

I take a deep breath and blurt out, "I slept with Nicholas, and he hasn't called me since he left Saturday morning. Now I'm feeling like I've been used for sex and tossed aside like an old shirt. Am I overthinking this? Emory thinks I should call him, but I can't. I just can't."

All of my words come out of my mouth like they're on some high-speed train racing toward some destination outside of me. I'm relieved to finally tell her what's on my mind, though.

"Wow, you slept with him? That's quick for you, Carey. He must be someone special to you."

Sighing, I lean back against my couch as I admit the truth to Jenna. "I thought he was. Why hasn't he called in two days? Is that a long time? Help me out here. I'm new to this century and its sexual ways."

I say that as a joke, but it just sounds sad. No wonder

both my best friends are shocked I slept with him so soon. They must secretly think I'm some pathetic prude stuck in the fifties with my attitude toward hooking up.

"It's not really two days."

"Fine. A day and a half. It feels the same."

"Do you really want my opinion?" Jenna asks, instantly scaring me.

She can be quite strident at times, especially about men, and I don't know if I can handle that right now. Perhaps the brutal, unvarnished truth isn't what's called for today.

"Can you soften it a little compared to your usual opinions? I'm feeling pretty vulnerable today."

"Okay. I can soften. Here's the thing, Carey. I just don't think this is a good time for you to be dating anyone, Nicholas or otherwise. Your boss was murdered and you found him. Then your ex-boyfriend was murdered. You're vulnerable right now because you have a lot of emotional stuff going on. So if this Nicholas guy used you, that's something you don't need to know. Don't call him like Emory said. Just let it lie, and if he's interested, he'll call. If not, it's his loss."

Her words sting, but at least she used a soft voice as she said them. "Okay. I get it."

"Men suck, Carey. I know Emory refuses to admit that, but they do. Accept that, and you'll be years ahead of the game."

Typical man-hating from Jenna, but I'm confused since she joined Emory to convince me I need to get out more. "I thought you said I needed to get out of my apartment and back into the dating scene."

"Well, yes, but as far as I'm concerned, I just wanted you to get out, not start dating men again. I'm not even sure you're over Chase yet. Not that he deserved you. Forget this Nicholas guy. Think of the sex as what it was. Good or bad, it was just sex."

Blowing the air out of my mouth, I'm not sure which of my friends I should listen to. Go with calling him and finding out once and for all like Emory said, or forgetting him and just sticking with my friends for a while like Jenna believes?

Either way, I'm still hoping Nicholas didn't sleep with me knowing he wanted nothing more.

Then she adds, "The thing is, Carey, you two might not be very compatible. Have you thought of that?"

Her comment hits me like a sharp slap to the face. "No," I barely mumble, feeling incredibly insecure at this moment. "I thought we had a lot in common."

"He's a wealthy businessman. You work as an assistant to the director of a toy museum. I'd bet you don't even make half of what he makes. What could you two have in common?"

I instantly want to defend myself since the way she described me made me sound like some poor, pathetic creature who should be thankful a man like Nicholas even paid the slightest attention to me. This isn't Jenna's typical man-hating, and I don't understand why she's saying these things.

Then again, maybe I do.

"We like each other, but that's not what this is about, is it?" I say, my voice shaky.

"If you don't want my opinion, don't ask, Carey. It's that simple," she snaps.

Taken aback by her brusque comment, I quietly say, "You haven't forgiven me yet, Jenna. I told you I swear I didn't think he was serious."

My mention of what her ex-fiancé said to me and my not telling her when I should have is followed by silence for so long I'm sure she's ended the call. I wouldn't bring up that topic at all, but she seems to be particularly unfeeling toward me today.

Finally, she says, "I don't know why you think anything we've talked about today has to do with him. Unless you're saying Nicholas is just like Christian. Is that what you mean? Because if that's the case and I find out about it, you better believe I'll be telling you about it."

And right there the truth comes out. She hasn't forgiven me.

"Jenna, I swear I thought he was joking. He was smiling when he told me, in passing I might add, that he might someday just pick up and vanish. I thought he was trying to be funny."

For the first time, her voice quivers when she says, "I don't care what you thought. When someone's fiancé says something like that, you tell them, Carey. I think I had the right to know he was even thinking something like that. The man took all my money and abandoned me. How do you think that feels?"

I wince at her description of what happened, even though I swear I didn't think he'd actually just pick up and vanish, leaving Jenna behind with not a cent to her name. I've tried more times than I can count to make her see I never meant to hurt her by not telling her what Christian said, but clearly, I haven't succeeded yet.

"Jenna, I'm sorry. I swear I still feel terrible about what happened. I thought he was a great guy. I never imagined he'd do such a horrible thing."

"Well, he wasn't."

We fall into an uncomfortable silence as I wish I could find a way to make her realize how awful I feel about what happened. If only I had never told her what he said when I found out about him leaving without a word.

"I guess I better go. I have to go back to work tomorrow. That ought to be great."

"Why? You love your job," Jenna says in a far sweeter voice than just a few moments ago.

I quickly debate whether or not to tell her about what Monica said at the memorial service. Jenna may still be angry with me, but I know deep down inside she's my friend.

"One of my co-workers caught me in the bathroom at the memorial service and mentioned she knew about Chase dying. I'm worried everyone at the museum knows by now and will look at me like I'm some kind of black widow or something."

"Do you really believe they'd think that? About you?"

"I'm the only connection between both Mr. James and my ex. Officer Thompson even brought it up, the charming individual he is."

Jenna groans. "Carey, if anyone says anything to you, just tell them if they don't shut their mouths, they're going to be next. That'll keep them from gossiping about you."

I can actually imagine Jenna saying exactly that and people being afraid of her. With my luck, I'd say those same words and not five minutes later, good old Officer Thompson would be showing up at my desk happy to put me in handcuffs and lead me off to jail based on nothing other than the fact that I've turned from a person being threatened to the one doing the threatening. I bet he'd love that too.

"Well, I think we both know I'm not going to say anything like that, but thanks for sticking up for me anyway. I better go. Do you have work today?"

That gets me another groan. "Yes, but I'm thinking about calling off. I have some things I need to take care of, and the last thing I want to deal with today is that damn sous chef. He's decided he doesn't want to make my life a living hell and has started hitting on me. What a tool. Maybe I wouldn't hate him if he hadn't made work suck so much from the moment he started working there. Not that it matters, but if he thinks I'm going to say yes to him asking me out, he's crazy."

That's Jenna for you. She'll be man-hating until her dying breath, if I know her.

I consider suggesting she give this guy a chance since they clearly have a few things in common working at the same restaurant, but I choose to not tilt at that windmill today. Better to let her enjoy her feelings against him after all the hassle he caused her.

Maybe she has the right idea with this hating men

thing. I just wish she could forgive that ex of hers so she could finally forgive me too.

AFTER CHECKING my phone nearly a million times yesterday and never seeing a missed call or text from Nicholas, I crawled into bed around five in the afternoon, pulling the covers up over my head and calling it a day. Somewhere around seven o'clock, I became militant and basically decided if he doesn't want me, then I don't want him. I faltered on that before nine p.m. after watching a sappy romance movie, but by the time I fell asleep at right after ten, I was as close to man-hating as I could get.

Jenna would be so proud.

This morning, however, I'm just hoping when I get out of my car that I'm not swarmed by co-workers curious to know why people keep dying around me, or worse, shunning me because they think I'm bad luck or cursed.

I look around and can't help but feel this place looks different than it usually does. That's probably just because I haven't been to work in over a week. I see the groundskeeper mowed the grass recently, and the pink and white flowers along the sidewalk that lead around the museum look better than ever.

I've missed being here. I just hope I feel that way when I leave to drive home at five tonight.

Feeling a little jittery, I take a deep breath to calm myself and slowly get out of the car. The drive here took less time than usual, so I'm early. That's not a bad thing, though, since I'm starting fresh with Michael as my boss today. Better to be in the office a few minutes before nine to make a good impression.

Sitting down at my desk, I'm feeling more than a little relieved. I saw three co-workers on my way here, and none of them looked at me in any way that seemed odd or judgmental. I was probably just worried about nothing.

Typical Carey stuff actually. If there's a way I can stress out over something, I find it and multiply it by ten.

I turn my computer on, and beside it, I see a sheet of paper with instructions about the benefit Mr. James left me. I must have missed it that day.

Briefly, I scan it and smile. He didn't have to worry about any of the issues he wrote down since I had taken care of everything. I see he even mentioned about the canapes, even though I specifically told him I spoke to the caterer and everything was set regarding them and all the other hors d'oeuvres.

Leave it to Mr. James to worry about nothing. He's worse than I am.

As I think that, I frown. Was worse than I am. He stressed out over so much, and none of it mattered in the end. Poor Mr. James.

That makes me wonder how Officer Thompson is doing with his investigation into my boss's murder, but the last thing I want to do today is talk to him. Make that the last thing I want to do any day is deal with that guy.

A knock on my door stirs me from my thoughts about my boss and the cop I'd like to never see again, and I look up to see Misha in my doorway. "Hey, you. How are you doing this fine Monday?"

I'd wondered how it would be working for her boss, but I hadn't considered what she'd be doing now that Michael has temporarily stepped into Mr. James's position. I'm glad it's not awkward between us.

"I'm good. Glad to be back. How are you?"

I don't ask what the situation is going to be for her now, even though I'm curious. Better to let her tell me herself.

"I'm good! Looks like we're going to be sharing Michael until the decision is made by the board as to who should be the director. Personally, I think he should get the job, but I'm not sure I want a new boss."

Since she seems to be in a good mood, I wave her in and say, "Close the door, okay?"

Now that Mr. James isn't here to impose his no closed door rule on me, I take advantage of the privacy to ask her about Michael since I really don't know him that well. He's always been pleasant, but I'd like to know a little more about him since he's now my boss too.

She sits down in the chair in front of my desk and leans forward, whispering, "What's up?"

I'm guessing she thinks I have some juicy gossip to share, but I quickly smile and shake my head. "Oh, nothing. We don't have to whisper. I just figured I should ask the woman who knows Michael better than anyone else around here what he's like to work for. I'm so used to Mr. James that I don't want to mess up with a new boss."

Misha rolls her eyes and chuckles as she waves off my concern. "Oh, you couldn't mess up with Michael. He's the sweetest guy in the world to work for. Do you know I don't think he's ever even raised his voice even a little bit in all the time I've worked for him?"

"Well, that's good to hear. Not that my old boss yelled much, but Mr. James was very serious about everything."

"That's not Michael. Trust me. He's mellow. I bet you're going to love the change."

As soon as she says that, a darkness fills her expression and she quickly adds, "Not that Mr. James was bad. I didn't mean it that way. Oh, God. I must sound like a horrible person talking about the dead like that. Don't tell anyone I said that, okay?"

I reach out and gently touch the top of her hand on the edge of my desk. "It's okay. You didn't say anything wrong. Michael is very different than Mr. James. Just being able to call my boss by his first name is a huge change. I do like that. It feels a little more casual, and I appreciate it."

Her entire body relaxes as I ease her mind about what she said. Misha's a wonderful person. Even if the entire museum staff heard her say that, they wouldn't think twice about it.

"Oh, thank you, Carey. I know it's been so hard for you, especially after being the person to find him upstairs. You're so strong to be able to come back to work like you have. I'm sure I'd be at home rocking myself back and forth on my couch watching old Oprah reruns for weeks if I had walked into that doll room like that. What a terrible thing to have to go through."

I nod, but I don't say anything in response. I know she's just trying to be sympathetic, but I don't want to think about finding Mr. James or that freaky doll storage room today. It's a fresh start for me with a new boss, and I want to focus on that.

"So other than letting me call him by his first name, is there anything else I should know about working for Michael?" I ask, aiming to redirect our conversation back to the original reason I asked her to come in to chat.

Misha looks up toward the ceiling as she thinks about her answer and then looks at me again. "No, I don't think so. He's super easy going, which I've always loved. I mean, I always get my work done on time, but if I need a day off, it's merely a matter of telling him when I can't come in. I just know you're going to be fine with him."

Not exactly what I was looking for, but maybe there's nothing for her to tell me. With other people, I might think they were holding back because of jealousy or insecurity, but not Misha. I guess he's just a great boss.

After all I've been through these past weeks, I can deal with that.

She looks at her watch and abruptly stands up. "Oh, I better go. I have to visit the ladies' room before the day starts. Too much coffee for me means I'm practically floating. Come to my office when you take a break this morning. I brought coffee cake I made yesterday. Oh, that is one thing. Michael has a terrible sweet tooth and always says he shouldn't eat what I make, but he always does. He never gains an ounce while I just look at sugar and my hips expand."

We both laugh as I make a mental note of Michael's love of sweet treats. Unfortunately, I'm not much of a baker just like I'm not a good cook, but maybe I could pick something up at that bakery near my house.

"Will do. Thanks!" I say as she hurries out of my office.

Glancing at the clock on the bottom left of my laptop screen, I see it's one minute to nine. I'd hoped to see Michael by now so he could notice I was early today, but so far he hasn't shown up.

Then again, maybe he isn't the type of boss who checks in on his executive assistant first thing every workday. That would be fine with me. I don't need much guidance to do my job. Why Mr. James never realized that I don't know.

For a few seconds, the horrible thought that maybe something has happened to Michael crosses my mind. Mr. James didn't come in that morning he was late, and he ended up dead, hanging from the ceiling surrounded by creepy doll heads.

Shaking my head, I push that thought out of my mind. "Don't be ridiculous," I whisper to myself. "Nobody is dead here today."

Talk about a weird way to cheer yourself up.

I start compiling the data for the report on the benefit I know Michael will want later this week, and a few minutes later, the man himself walks into my office wearing a huge smile. I immediately notice he isn't wearing a tie with his white dress shirt and gray suit. Mr. James would never come to work without a tie.

It's a nice change to see my boss so relaxed.

"Good morning, Carey. I wanted to stop in to say hi and let you know I'll be in and out of the office all this week."

Before I can say a word to him, my office phone

begins to ring. We stare at each other, him probably wondering why I don't answer it, and me unsure if I should since Mr. James never liked when I interrupted his visits by answering the phone. He always said whoever it was would call back. That seemed like an odd thought for a man who wanted more than anything to make the museum a success, but in all likelihood, very few people who could help this place grow would be calling me instead of him.

"Is there a reason you aren't answering that?"

I open my mouth to explain and then close it again, unsure I should bring up my former boss. He wasn't fired or let go in disgrace, though. The man died, and even though it was under horrible circumstances, I'm sure Michael won't mind me telling him the truth.

"Mr. James never liked me to answer the phone when he was in my office. I guess old habits die hard."

Oh, God. I used the word die in the same thought as Mr. James.

Michael's expression doesn't show he noticed, so I quickly say, "I just don't know what your policy is on that. That's all."

He smiles and points at the phone on the corner of my desk. "It's fine. We're all going to be getting used to things for a while. You answer that, and I'll go find Misha. I hear she brought in a coffee cake I shouldn't eat but will. We can talk later."

Relieved, I reach for my phone and say, "Thanks, Michael."

I barely get the receiver to my ear when I hear Emory

already talking. "...and I thought you should know. Oh my God, Carey! What is going on?"

Michael hears her talking so loudly I'm sure people in the hallway heard that too and stops dead right before he gets to my door. I have no idea what she's talking about, but now that I've answered the phone, I have to at least tell her I'll call her back.

"Emory, I'm with my boss right now. Can I call you later?"

"Oh, yeah. Okay. I just thought you should know about him being in the hospital. I'm starting to get worried, though, Carey."

Now I can't just hang up without asking her what she means by that, so I quietly say as professionally as possible, "What are you talking about, Emory?"

"Nicholas! Your guy was attacked last night. I just saw it on the local news. You know, the one with the anchor who has the hair that looks like someone took a hand mixer to it and made it like cotton candy? I was watching it as I had my morning coffee before I try to get that damn muse of mine to cooperate, and she said Nicholas Madera, local businessman, was attacked coming out of his penthouse on Sunday night. He's in the hospital in critical condition!"

As Michael stares at me probably wondering what's wrong, I feel like my office walls are starting to close in on me. A third man I know? But he was only attacked? Thank God.

"Carey, are you there? Did you hear what I said? What is going on?" Emory asks frantically.

"I don't know. I have to call you back, okay?" I say, hanging up without even remembering to say goodbye.

My hands shake uncontrollably as I sit back in disbelief. Michael walks over to my desk and stops next to it. "What's wrong?"

"A friend of mine is in the hospital. Someone attacked him when he was leaving his house last night. My friend Emory called to let me know. She says he's in critical condition at the hospital," I say flatly, unsure what could be happening.

"Do you need to go?" Michael asks.

I look up at him and practically burst into tears at how wonderful that question sounds. My old boss would have been irritated someone interrupted my workday with such emotional baggage.

"Would it be okay? To be honest, I'm not sure how much work I'll be able to get done after hearing that. I'm sorry, Michael. This is no way to start out a new working relationship with you."

He shakes his head and gives me a look like that's the dumbest thing he's ever heard. "Not at all. It's okay. Go see your friend."

As I stand up from behind my desk, I say, "It's Nicholas Madera. I met him at the benefit. He's a huge supporter of the museum."

The look Michael gives me is pure confusion, like he can't understand why yet another person associated with me has been hurt. And he doesn't even know about Chase. Or maybe he does.

Oh, God. Officer Thompson is right, at least with the

part about my being the only connection between the people killed and now with Nicholas.

Whatever's going on, I'm just so happy they didn't succeed a third time.

22

"He's at Campion," Emory says as I drive out of the museum parking lot holding the steering wheel in one hand and my phone in the other.

"What else did they say? Do they know who did it? How bad is he? Critical condition is bad. What happened?" I ask in Gatling gun fashion while I speed down the road toward where Campion Hospital is a few miles away.

"All I heard the cotton candy lady say is he was in critical condition after being attacked just outside his building. She said it happened late Sunday night."

"Thank God he's okay. Jesus, Emory. What the fuck is going on here? You have to see that all three—Mr. James, Chase, and now Nicholas—all three of them only have me in common. Someone is trying to terrorize me through them. That seems like an odd thing to do considering who I am."

"What does that mean?" Emory asks, sounding almost insulted for me.

"It means I'm not exactly the girl who's the most popular with the opposite sex. Mr. James and I were only co-workers, so there was no sexual relationship there, but still. The other two men I know in the biblical sense. Do you think that has something to do with this?"

She doesn't answer for a long moment as I make a lefthand turn to get onto the road where the hospital is located. Unsure if the call dropped, I pull the phone away from my ear and see it's still a live call.

"Emory? You aren't saying anything."

"I'm not sure what to say. I thought it was weird when Chase was murdered in the same way your boss was, but I didn't say anything. Maybe it was just a terrible coincidence. But this makes me really wonder. The good thing is Nicholas is still alive, so maybe he can tell the cops what the attacker looked like."

My heart sinks as she says that. I knew I wasn't the only person worried that connection between Mr. James and Chase pointed to me.

"But why would anyone want to hurt people who know me?"

Again, she takes a long time before answering. "I'm not sure, honey, but I think it's possible you have an enemy."

"What are you saying? That whoever is doing this wants me to be blamed for Mr. James and Chase's deaths?"

This time she doesn't hesitate to answer. "And Nicholas's, if he hadn't survived. Thank God he did. I'm worried, Carey. Maybe you should come stay with me until this is all over."

All I can think of when she suggests that is she'll be the next victim if I do as she wants.

"I need you to promise me you'll be careful, okay, Emory? I don't know what's going on, but if some person is going after people I know, you might be in danger. Call Jenna and tell her that. I would if I had the time, but I'm almost to the hospital. God, I hope they let me see him. I just have to know he's okay."

"I will. I'll call Jenna right after I get off the phone with you. Promise me you'll be careful too, though. Just because it seems like someone is going after people you know doesn't mean they won't turn around and go after you."

As much as I want to think she's wrong, I know from what those horrible letters said that it's possible. It's just that all of this feels like some nightmare I can't wake up from, and for someone who never has nightmares, this first one is downright terrifying.

"Okay. I will," I say as I see the hospital straight up ahead at the top of a small hill. "I'm here. I'll call you after I see him, assuming they let me."

"Good luck," Emory says sweetly. "Let me know if you need me to do anything, okay?"

"Thanks. I will."

I WAIT AT THE NURSES' station for permission to see Nicholas after being told he's no longer in critical condition. Never in my life have I been so relieved.

And guilty. If I'm the connection to all these crimes

like Officer Thompson thinks, then I'm partly to blame for Nicholas being attacked.

So much for thinking he was a lowdown son of a bitch who sleeps with women and never calls again. He's not the villain. I might be.

I can't think about that now. If I do, I'll fall apart right here on the third floor of this hospital and create a scene, which is the last thing I want to do.

A big woman in a white nurse uniform with bright red hair waves me over to her, so I hurry to where she's standing at the end of the nurses' station. After smiling at me, she pats me gently on the shoulder.

"You can go in. Room six. He's doing better, but don't get him excited."

I'm not sure if that's a sex joke or she thinks I'm his girlfriend, but I don't say anything and simply nod before walking to the room. I don't go in at first, unsure I should even be here since I'm not a relative and I've only known him for a couple weeks.

What if he doesn't want to see me since he didn't call me after we had sex?

I remind myself he's been in the hospital since Sunday night, which means he couldn't have called me even if he wanted to. But none of that matters. All I care about is seeing he's okay.

Cautiously, I poke my head into the room and find him awake in bed wearing a blue hospital gown. Unsure what to say, I clear my throat and hope he looks in my direction.

"Carey?"

A horrible thought flashes through my mind. Does he have a head injury and doesn't remember me?

I nod and take a single step into his hospital room. "Yes, it's me, Nicholas. I just heard you were attacked. I wanted to come see how you're doing."

He gives me a big smile, but it can't hide the bruises down the right side of his face and all around his neck. Oh, God! Did someone try to strangle him? That would be just like they did with Mr. James and Chase.

"You must be furious with me, but you came here anyway."

I take another step into his room and stop, unsure what he means. "Why would I be angry?"

Groaning, he eases himself up against the pillow and let's out a heavy sigh like that single action took every ounce of energy he has in his body. "I didn't call you after the other night. For what it's worth, I was planning on calling today, but I'm a little preoccupied at the moment."

So happy he's going to be okay and even happier he isn't a love 'em and leave 'em type like Emory thought he might be, I walk over to his bed and lightly touch his arm as I smile in utter joy. "It's okay. I wasn't sure for a while there, but it's fine. I guess what Mr. James said to me that night of the benefit really got into my head. If he were here now, I'd want to tell him where he can put his cryptic warnings."

Nicholas draws in his eyebrows at my mention of Mr. James's warning. "What did he say?"

"Oh, he just said to be careful after he saw me talking to you. I think he thought I wasn't rich enough to be with someone like you."

His expression softens, and Nicholas chuckles. "No, that's not what he meant at all. He told you to be careful because he never got over the fact that I dated his wife first, and she never let him forget it."

What? Not only did Mr. James have a wife who died, but now I learn she used to date Nicholas too? So my boss's warning was simple jealousy?

"You and Mrs. James? I had no idea! Then again, I had no idea there even was a Mrs. James, so I've clearly been out of the loop. So that's why he was so miserable about you."

Nodding, Nicholas says, "She wasn't Mrs. James at the time. She was just Elise. We were only friends after we broke up, but he never believed that. He was sure she was cheating on him with me, no matter what I said to the contrary. I had hoped when she passed that he'd let those feelings of jealousy go with her, but every so often they reared their ugly heads. That night at the benefit must have been one of those times."

I'm stunned by all that he's told me about my old boss. Who knew Mr. James could be so sordid and petty? I guess since I knew nothing about his personal life, none of this should shock me, but it does. He was the picky guy who fussed and stressed about the museum to me. Now that I know so much more about his life outside of work, I have to admit he's not the man I thought he was.

"So how are you feeling? What happened? I couldn't believe when my friend told me she heard on the news you were attacked."

I sit down in the chair next to his bed and realize he may not want to talk about this right now. "I'm sorry. I'm acting like that cop who keeps pestering me. Forget I asked any of that. We can talk about whatever you want or not talk at all. Or I can leave. You're the patient, so it's your call."

Nicholas slowly moves his arm as he reaches for my hand, and the first touch of his warm skin on mine brings back memories of our night together. I smile and see he's smiling too.

"It's okay, Carey. It's only natural to ask what happened. I'm not really sure, to be honest. I walked out of my building to go to my car parked in the garage. I made some small talk with the doorman about the baseball game last night, and the next thing I knew, someone jumped me."

"Probably trying to rob you," I say, hoping he might agree with me.

But he doesn't.

Shaking his head, he says, "Not likely. They tried to strangle me. Muggers don't generally do things that way."

My heart sinks at hearing him say that. Now there's no way to deny the truth. Whoever murdered Mr. James and Chase tried to do the same thing to Nicholas. That they were unsuccessful doesn't change the fact that they wanted to kill him.

But why? And am I really the thread tying all these men together?

He gently squeezes my hand and tears me out of my thoughts. "It's okay. I'm going to be fine."

Feeling like I need to tell him about everything, I say, "Nicholas, I think I'm the reason you were attacked."

It sounds like a ridiculous claim, and he looks at me

like he's completely baffled at my announcement. "Is there a jealous husband I should know about?" he asks and then smiles.

"No, nothing like that. I wish it was as easy as that."

I really don't want to admit that two people I know have been murdered by strangulation. It's bad enough he knows about my boss.

Nicholas waits for me to continue, and since there's no point in stopping now, I go ahead and tell him the entire truth. When I finish explaining that Mr. James and Chase were both strangled and both found with dolls' heads nearby, I'm too afraid to look into his eyes in the fear that I'll see utter disgust.

He doesn't say anything for a long time, so I finally lift my eyes to meet his gaze. "I didn't know how to tell you or even if I should. I guess in hindsight it's pretty obvious with the dolls and the strangulation, but I swear I really didn't know what to say to people about it. I mean, why on earth would anyone want to attack people I know? It makes no sense."

Finally, he smiles and says, "It's okay, Carey. I'm not sure we were at that point in our relationship where you'd want to tell me anything like that."

"I would never want to hurt you or anyone, Nicholas. I hope you know that. I'll understand if you don't want to see me again because of this, but please know I never meant you any harm."

"Of course, I know that. You couldn't hurt a fly."

I hang my head and sigh. "Maybe you could tell the cops that. I think that Officer Thompson is convinced I'm the criminal mastermind behind the deaths of Mr. James and my ex. I fully expect to be hauled into the police station now that you've been attacked because whoever did this tried to strangle you."

"That won't be necessary," a voice behind me says, and I turn around to see Officer Thompson standing in the doorway to the hospital room.

"May I come in, Mr. Madera? I'd like to ask you some questions."

I quickly stand to leave, sure I don't want to endure watching someone I care about being grilled by this irritating man. Would it really hurt to give Nicholas a day to rest up from his attack?

"Don't go, Carey," he says, still holding my hand.

As much as I want to be anywhere but in the vicinity of Officer Thompson, I smile and sit down again. The police officer who's become a constant in my life lately stands on the other side of the room leaning against the wall near the windows, and I watch him take out that all-too-familiar little notepad of his.

"I spoke to the police earlier, officer," Nicholas says. "I should also tell you that I'm one hundred percent sure it wasn't Carey here who attacked me."

Officer Thompson smiles, and for a moment, he looks like a nice guy. That quickly passes, however, and he says, "I know it wasn't. Despite what she may think, I don't believe it's her who's been killing and attacking people."

I have to bit my tongue to not snap, "How nice."

"Do you know who attacked you, Mr. Madera?"

"No, but I can describe them. It was dark, but I got a look at the person. I'm guessing they were about five eight. Maybe a little taller, but not much. And I think it was a woman."

Officer Thompson lifts his head and stops writing in his notebook. "A woman did this to you? Any chance it's a girlfriend or an angry ex?"

I think I truly hate this man. I really and truly do.

As much as I want to glare at him, I work to keep my expression emotionless so he can't see his question bothers me. Maybe it's jealousy, or maybe it's the way he said that while Nicholas and I sit here holding hands.

Or maybe it's just because I can't stand Officer Thompson.

Nicholas takes the question in stride and smiles as he shakes his head. "No, I don't think it's an ex, and since the only woman I'm dating is sitting right here and I just told you I'm one hundred percent sure it wasn't her, I'm afraid that line of questioning isn't going to get you very far."

Officer Thompson looks at me when Nicholas informs him we're a couple and then jots down something in his notepad. Probably some comment about me being dangerous to men or something sexist like that.

"Okay, but you do think it was a woman?" he asks after he finishes writing his note. "Why?"

"Because they came at me from behind, and I felt breasts pressing against me," Nicholas answers. "Now it could be a fat man, but the person wasn't that big. I think it was a woman. Not an ex and not Carey. I wish I could be more specific, but it was dark and it happened very fast. One minute I was walking through the parking garage at my building to go to my car, and the next thing I knew someone had their hands around my neck and were trying to choke the life out of me."

The officer nods and writes more notes before looking up and asking, "Did they wear gloves or were they barehanded?"

"Gloves. I remember distinctly the feel of leather on my neck."

"Did you black out from them choking you?"

Nicholas shakes his head. "No. I pushed them off me, and then I was hit over the head and knocked out. And before you ask me with what, all I can tell you is it was hard and the goose egg on the back of my head feels like it's the size of a softball."

He winces after saying that and then turns to look at me. "You should feel this thing. It's huge!" he says with a chuckle.

Officer Thompson isn't interested in joking, so he doesn't miss a beat and asks, "Is there anything else you remember?"

Blowing the air out of his mouth, Nicholas thinks for a moment or two and says, "You know what? I forgot to mention this to the other officer, but now that you ask, there is something else. It's weird, but I remember the smell of French fries. You know that greasy food smell that clings to your clothes if you're around it for too long? I don't know. Maybe that has nothing to do with anything because I was going out to grab some food through the drive-thru when it happened."

The officer takes down what he says anyway, and then closes his notebook. "Okay, I'll let you enjoy your visit with Miss Mitchell. If you remember anything else, please call me."

He sets his business card on the table next to the bed and smiles. "Miss Mitchell, I hope you're keeping yourself safe. More and more, this is looking like it all has to do with you."

Nice of him to scare the hell out of me before walking out.

"He's a little slice of heaven right here on earth, isn't he?" I say after he leaves.

Nicholas laughs and then winces from pain. "He definitely is a by-the-book kind of guy, but I think most cops are. Now that I'm done with my second police interview of the day, what do you say we have a date right here and now in this hospital room? The food here isn't great, and the TV only gets a couple channels, but we don't care about that, do we?"

I lift his hand to my mouth and press a kiss to his fingers. "I don't care about any of that. I'm good with just the two of us hanging out for a while."

"Me too."

23

Do you think one mishap is going to make me stop? Think again. I'm not done yet. Not by a long shot.

That guy should have died. I felt his heartbeat begin to slow as I squeezed the life out of him. He fought hard, but I'm surprisingly strong for my size. It only would have taken another minute or two and he would have been dead.

If it wasn't for that car backfiring and making me lose my focus, he would be dead. Victim number three. I had the doll's head ready to leave by his body and everything. It was all planned out.

I have to admit he put up more of a struggle than the first two. That museum guy wasn't much to handle. He couldn't have weighed more than a hundred and sixty pounds soaking wet. All those hours fixating over the proper way to exhibit a goddamned Slinky or a can of Play-Doh doesn't leave much time for working out.

So it didn't take much to strangle the life out of him. Hanging him from the ceiling took a little work, but I'm not a person who doesn't put one hundred percent into a task. You should see me at my job. They all know me as someone who's all in whenever I have a task to complete.

The second one was even easier. You see, he invited me into his car. What a dog he was. He actually thought we were going to get down to business and he'd get his jollies with me in the back seat.

So I climbed behind him as he drove to that parking lot, and as soon as he turned off the car, I made my move. He actually thought it was foreplay for a few seconds there. Jesus, men can be so stupid. Get a little blood flowing between their legs and they can't see what's obviously happening to them.

It was remarkably simple to kill him. I expected him to honk the horn or something to get someone's attention, but he never did. His flailed his arms and tried to scream, but it's surprisingly difficult to get any sound out when someone is pressing hard enough on your windpipe to crush it.

So he fought a little, but the end result was never in doubt.

When he stopping fighting the inevitable and went limp against the seat, I knew I'd succeeded once again. I fished that creepy ass doll's head out of the bag I had with me and tossed it onto the passenger seat.

You may be thinking that I must have left fingerprints all over that car, so the police will surely be able to figure out who killed him. Highly unlikely. You see, he had so many women in that car and the amount of junk he had all over the floor told me he rarely, if ever, cleaned the damn thing. I guess they can haul all of us in, but you know how it is with fingerprints.

If you haven't committed a crime or ever been fingerprinted, how would the police know who's been in that car?

Just in case you're wondering, I've never been caught killing anyone, and I've never had my fingerprints taken. My job doesn't require that. So they'll never figure out I was there.

So that brings us to the current moment. Victim number three didn't pan out as I wanted him to, but I'm not a person who gives up, so he should keep an eye out. But for what? He never saw me or heard my voice. There's nothing even remotely distinguishable about me. That's the beauty of this whole thing.

I'm the last person you'd ever think would do such terrible things.

But are they really that terrible? Let's be honest. All three of them deserved it. That Randall James guy was a complete shit to you. He worked you far harder than anyone else in that silly museum. You were his gopher, his Girl Friday, his punching bag when he got upset about anything. For God's sake, he had rules about every damn part of the job that you had to follow or he'd lecture you for hours.

Anyway, not a damn soul misses him. Not even you.

And Chase? Please. He cheated on you and broke your heart. And that was only with one girl you knew about! Trust me. There were dozens more. You really were quite the patsy when it came to him, weren't you? I mean, the signs were all there. Obvious and as clear as the nose on your face. All the times he didn't call when he was supposed to. All the times he showed up hours late. Seriously, honey, you chose to be blind to what you had to know was happening.

Admit it. Somewhere deep inside where you don't want to think about and where you push your darkest insecurities down to, you knew he was cheating on you constantly. Good riddance to him is what I say.

As for number three, he's no better. He's going to do to you what that last one did. He's already starting, isn't he? You finally took a chance and slept with someone without it being a serious relationship, and he never called after he got you in bed. That's all he wanted, isn't it? You know that's the truth.

He's just like every other man. He got what he wanted, and then he disappeared. No call. No flowers. Nothing. Just wham, bam, thank you ma'am, but he never said thanks, now did he?

I don't plan on stopping, so get ready because there will be another victim. It's not like the cops are actually going to be able to stop me. They've been thinking it's you all this time. Didn't you realize that? They actually thought you, little Carey who lives in some old-fashioned world where good guys and girls don't finish last, truly is capable of killing someone.

Maybe I'll kill that officer just because he's been stupid for too long.

Stay tuned.

24

I STARE at the letter in my hand and shake my head in disbelief. Who is this person, and why are they doing this to me and the people I care about? What did I do to whoever this is to deserve this?

The logical side of my brain says to immediately call Officer Thompson. This is a letter from the killer, and this one might actually give him a clue as to who's behind everything.

Still, I can't stand the idea of dealing with him right now. I can't bear his suspicious looks when he asks me questions. Not today. Not after seeing Nicholas lying in that hospital bed after someone attacked him.

Maybe later. Right now, I need to be around friends who love me and don't look at me like I'm some kind of criminal myself.

I grab my phone and call Emory, hoping the muse is still a no-show so she can come over and hang out. She answers quickly, which I think might be a good sign.

"Tell me everything you found out!" she says right off the bat without even saying hello.

"First, I want you to come over today and hang out with me. I know you're working, and ordinarily I wouldn't ask something like this, but I'm needing my friends right now. Can you come over?"

Emory sighs. "Can I come over in about two hours? I met someone last night, and he just left a few minutes ago. I'd love to get a little work done today so I don't feel like a completely useless artist. Say about two?"

Slightly disappointed, I, of course, agree. "Sure. But who's the guy? Why didn't you tell me before you were with someone?"

"Because I had just found out the last guy you slept with was on the TV after being attacked. I was a little busy thinking about that, and anyway, he was lying right next to me. I couldn't exactly tell you how he rocked my world and that I planned to have another go with him before he had to leave," Emory says, giggling.

"Okay, you're forgiven, but now you have to spill the details."

"I'll tell you when I get there at two. Right now, let me go so I can get some work done, or you're going to be talking to the newest member of the crew at Walmart because I'm too poor to pay my bills. I'll see you at two. Want me to bring anything? This isn't going to be a sobfest kind of visit, is it? Nicholas is going to be okay, isn't he?"

I can't help but smile when she says his name. "Yes, he's going to be okay. The news exaggerated, I think. He's not in critical condition, but he's sore after someone tried to strangle him and then hit him over the head to knock him out. And he was thrilled to see me and said he was planning to call, but you know, he was attacked."

"Oh, Carey! That's great! Okay, save any more details until I get there. Are you inviting Jenna too? She may have to go into work, though, because I know she had last night off."

That's odd. Jenna never gets Sundays off, especially since the new owners took over the restaurant. On top of the dozens of new rules they imposed the moment they walked through the door, they decided to require everyone to work Fridays, Saturdays, and Sundays. She's hated that change the most.

"Really? Did she get a special dispensation from the Pope for that? Her new bosses have been total hardasses about weekends for the entire staff."

Emory curses after knocking something over and says, "Yeah, I don't know. I don't think the Pope was involved, but I don't remember if she told me why she had the night off. She had to work during the day, though, so maybe that's what happened."

Then I remember what Jenna said about that sous chef hitting on her. "Oh, yeah. She mentioned something about maybe taking last night off. I must not have realized it was Sunday. God, these past few weeks I don't know if I'm coming or going."

"Well, I have to go. I've got a mess to clean up, and then I have to do some work, so I'll see you at two, okay?"

She ends the call before I can say okay or goodbye, so I immediately call Jenna. She answers quickly too.

"Hey, you! What's up? Things any better on the man front?"

I hesitate to dump all the news of what's happened into her lap, so I just say, "Yeah, I think so. Do you want to come over this afternoon and hang out with Emory and me? She's getting here at two. I just want to have my friends around me today."

Without thinking about my suggestion, she says, "Yeah! But first, let's grab a bite to eat. I'm starving, and unless something big has changed in your life and your refrigerator, there's nothing to snack on at your place, right?"

My dear friend knows me well.

Chuckling, I say, "Yeah, pretty much."

"Then I'll pick you up in five, and we'll grab something small before stopping at the store to load up on snacks for when Emory joins us at two. See you in a few!"

Excited for an afternoon with my friends, I ask, "Do you have work tonight, or do we get you until the cows come home?"

She laughs at my using that phrase and answers, "I don't have work until tomorrow night, so it's the three musketeers riding together again tonight. Look out world!"

"Emory had a guy spend the night last night, so be prepared. I'm going to be asking for details."

I know how much she can get her man-hating groove on at times, so I want to give her fair warning. Jenna can be difficult about men since that fiancé of hers practically ruined her life, but I suspect she loves listening to Emory's sexy stories as much as I do.

Jenna groans into the phone. "Ugh, really? She wanted me to go out with her, but I had to beg off. I thought she was staying in and bitching out that muse of hers, but I guess she went out on the prowl instead."

"Yeah, well he stayed until this morning when she called me. I'll tell you all about that when you pick me up. Hey, by the way, she said you didn't have to work last night. Are your new owners softening up?"

"Uh, yeah. You know how bosses are. Yours used to be a doozy, right? Let me go, and I'll be there in a couple."

Her mention of Mr. James puts a damper on my mood for a few seconds, but I force myself to be happy again and tell her I'll be ready when she gets here. Today's a day for happiness, so no being sad. Nicholas is going to be fine, and my best friends and I are going to have a good old-fashioned girls' day together. I don't want to think about murder or threatening letters for at least a few hours.

After a quick bite at Jenna's favorite taco joint and paying for a few to take with us, we head back to my apartment to meet Emory at two. We still have forty-five minutes, so I say to her, "Do you mind stopping at the hospital? Nicholas isn't being released until tomorrow morning, assuming his CT scan went okay, so I'd love to pop in and just say hi."

She turns to look at me and shakes her head. "Girl, you're already lost on this one, aren't you? That sex must have been pretty good. I guess him not calling the next day and breaking one of your cardinal rules isn't a big deal anymore?"

I know she's poking fun at me, so I just laugh. "I'm not that rigid that I can't give a guy a break. He was attacked by some maniac, for God's sake."

"Not the day after, right?"

"True, but I'm feeling forgiving today. Can we stop at the hospital? I promise it won't be for long. Just a few minutes and then we'll leave. I just want to say hi, see how he's doing, and maybe surprise him with a taco or two. He says the food there isn't great."

She stops at a light and throws her head back in laughter. "Of course it isn't! It's hospital food. Okay, off we go to see Carey's new Mr. Right!"

JENNA and I stop just outside Nicholas's hospital room. Taking the bag of tacos from her, I put it behind my back.

"I want to surprise him."

She gives me a look like she thinks I'm pathetic, but that's okay. That's just Jenna. I know her. She won't say anything in front of him to embarrass me. She keeps her negativity about guys to when it's just Emory and me around.

Nicholas lights up when he sees me walk into the room followed by Jenna. "Twice in one day? I hope this doesn't mean I'm in worse shape than I thought."

Pulling the bag out from behind my back, I say, "Surprise! We went for tacos, and I thought since the food here isn't to your liking that you'd enjoy a couple. You're not on any dietary restrictions, are you? I didn't even think about that when I decided to bring you these."

He reaches out and takes the bag from me. "None whatsoever. They're just keeping me to make sure my brains aren't completely scrambled."

Lost in how happy he looks as he slides those two tacos out of the bag, I forget I'm not alone. Jenna walks up behind me and clears her throat, suddenly making me realize I'm being rude.

"Oh, I'm so sorry. Nicholas, this is my friend Jenna. Jenna, Nicholas Madera."

Like the gentleman he is, he extends his hand to shake hers, so she moves around me and leans in to shake it. I watch, thinking how sweet he is and how I could definitely fall in love with this man. Even laid up in a hospital bed, he's still charming and polite.

And gorgeous, even with all those bruises.

I watch his expression grow dark, but it's quickly replaced by a smile I know he's forcing. Oh, God. He's probably in pain right now, and here I am bringing strangers in to meet him.

Quickly, I move to fix my mistake. "Okay, we're going to go. I just wanted to stop in with the tacos, but you should get some rest. How about I call you later, okay?"

Nicholas nods, and still forcing that smile, he says, "Yeah, that'll be good. Nice to meet you, Jenna."

"Same. Feel better soon."

I hurry out of that hospital room feeling like such an insensitive boob. How could I have thought he'd want to entertain guests after being attacked less than twenty-four hours ago? God, I hope he doesn't hate me now.

Jenna doesn't say much on the ride to my apartment, and I remain silent, lost in thought that I just ruined what was shaping up to be a great thing with him. Who the hell wants to be with a woman who can't figure out he doesn't want to meet new people when he's stuck in a hospital bed with a goose egg the size of a softball on the back of his head and bruises on his face and neck after some madman tried to kill him?

I'll be lucky if Nicholas even answers the phone when I call later.

I TOSS my house keys onto the kitchen counter and turn to look at Jenna as she sits down on one of the chairs in my living room. "Do you mind if I grab a shower? I feel like shit, all of a sudden. I think the taco grease is doing a number on me."

"Sure! I'll just watch some TV. Take your time."

My mind filled with regret, I head into the shower and hope I can wash away how awful I feel. This is why I'm single while Emory meets guys and has a great time as I sit in my apartment night after night watching bad TV.

If I'm not careful, I'm going to end up like Jenna hating men. No, that won't happen. I'll just hate myself.

25

FEELING REFRESHED FROM MY SHOWER, I get dressed and throw my hair into a ponytail, ready to enjoy some time with my two best friends. Checking my cell phone, I see it's nearly two o'clock.

Perfect timing.

"Emory should be here at any minute," I call out from my bedroom, hoping Jenna can hear me. "Better break out the chips. If her muse has been as difficult as I think she has, she's going to need a bag to herself."

She doesn't answer, which tells me I didn't yell loud enough. No matter. I can do my imitation of Big Ben when I get out to the living room.

I grab my cell and see a number I don't recognize called me. They can wait until later. It's probably some telemarketer anyway. I'll end up calling them back tomorrow and hear some message about them trying to contact me about my car's warranty.

"Do you ever get those stupid calls from whatever company that is that's trying to sell you a warranty for your car? I swear I get them at least twice a month," I say as I walk out to the kitchen.

Again, Jenna doesn't answer, and when I look into the living room, she's not there. Where could she be?

My apartment isn't that big, so I quickly look around, but I can't find her. Immediately, I begin to worry. The letter writer said he wasn't done. What if he came here to slip another letter under my door and ran into Jenna?

"I need you to come out right now, okay?" I call out in a shaky voice. "Seriously, Jenna. This isn't funny. Where are you?"

I return to my living room and see a note on the chair I never sit on. My heart pounding in my chest from utter terror, I walk over to it and pick it up, my hand shaking like a leaf in a storm.

Instantly, relief fills me. It's from Jenna telling me she ran out to the store to pick up stuff to make pizza bagels.

Collapsing onto that chair, I take a deep breath as why I never sit here comes rushing back to me in the form of a sharp pain in my lower back. The salesman at the furniture store said it was all the rage somewhere in Europe, and Emory convinced me to buy it, but I've never liked it since it came into my apartment. It sits there as decoration most of the time, unless Jenna's here since she somehow loves it.

A few minutes later, she walks in all smiles with grocery bags full of pizza bagel fixings. Holding them up like they're trophies, she says, "I had to fight some lady for the last everything bagel. Emory better eat it. I'm not hearing anything about that new diet she's on today."

"I'm sure she will. She's trying to eat healthier, but

everything bagels are her kryptonite," I say as I follow her into the kitchen.

She tosses her bag and the grocery bags onto the counter and turns to face me. "That iced tea from lunch is haunting me, so I'll help you put this stuff away as soon as I get back from the bathroom. I got mozzarella and some cheese Kraft claims is pizza cheese. I'll be right back."

Jenna rushes to the bathroom, and I start unloading the goodies she bought. It takes me no time to get everything put away, so once I stuff the plastic grocery bags into the bigger plastic bag I have hanging on the inside of my broom closet, I grab her canvas tote bag she uses since she hates purses and head to the living room to wait for her and Emory.

I toss the bag on that purgatorial chair and watch in horror as everything inside spills out onto the cushion. Hurrying over, I open it up to put it all back in and see something that makes my blood run cold.

A doll's head.

Instantly, I freeze in place, staring at the terrible thing. There's no reason she should have one of those in her bag. Who the hell carries around a doll's head in their bag?

My stomach twists into a tight knot because I know the answer.

A mixture of fear and sadness fills me, but my phone rings, so I pull it out of my pocket to see it's Nicholas. I quickly answer, unsure what to do but needing to tell someone what I just found.

"Carey, I need you to get to the police station right now. You're in danger," he says, sounding frantic.

"Why? What happened?"

"It's your friend. Jenna. She's the person who tried to kill me last night. I realized it when she shook my hand earlier at my hospital room. I smelled that same odor as I did last night when she was trying to strangle me."

What he said to Officer Thompson makes sense now. It wasn't French fries he was talking about. It's the smell everyone who works in a restaurant has on them after a shift. I'm so used to it because I've known her the entire time she's worked there, but that's it.

It's Jenna who's killing people in my life. But why?

"I know. I just found something in her bag that told me it's her. What do I do?" I ask, confused and frightened about what my next step should be.

"Where are you?"

"My apartment. We're having a girls' day in with snacks and pizza bagels. My friend Emory is due here at any moment."

"Get out of there right now! She's a killer, Carey. You're in real danger. I'm going to call the police, and I'll be there as soon as I can."

What's he talking about? He's in the hospital with a head injury. He can't go anywhere until the release him tomorrow.

"How can you be coming here? You're a patient in the hospital, Nicholas."

"Carey, just get out of there! I'm calling the police now. Just get out and go to your car or somewhere else she can't get to you. I'll be there in a few minutes."

The call ends, and it's like my head is swimming. One of my best friends is a murderer, and I'm alone with her in my apartment. This can't be happening.

"Who was that?" Jenna asks when she stops just a few steps into the living room.

Oh, God! I can't tell her the truth. She'll know something's wrong, and I don't know what she'll do if she gets upset or angry.

"Emory. She called to say she's going to be late."

Jenna shakes her head. "You're lying. It was that Nicholas guy, wasn't it? What did he say?" she asks, her expression darker than I've ever seen it before.

"Nothing. Nothing at all. He just wanted to tell me he loved the tacos. That's all."

She levels her gaze on my face and groans. "I knew I should have kept hitting him after he went down. If it wasn't for that asshole with his backfiring car, your new boyfriend would be dead just like the other two jackasses."

I step around the chair I hate and stand behind it, foolishly thinking having it in front of me provides some protection. It makes no sense, but I don't know what to do, and I'm scared out of my wits right now.

If only Nicholas and the police would get here.

"Why, Jenna? Mr. James and Chase never did anything to you. Neither did Nicholas. You just met him for the first time today. How could you want to kill him?" I ask, my voice trembling as I try not to cry.

"Because all three of them deserved it!" she yells so loud I jump in fear. "But even more, you deserved it."

I shake my head, not understanding. "Why? I'm your friend."

She stares at me like she's looking right through me. "I thought you were my friend. Some friend you turned out to be, Carey. You knew Christian was going to leave me, and you did nothing. Did you tell me? Did you say to him he shouldn't because I loved him? Did you do anything? Anything at all? No!"

This can't be happening. "I'm sorry. I honestly didn't think anything of it when he said all those things. I thought he was kidding."

That only enrages her more, and I see pure hate in her eyes now.

"He stole everything I had. He broke my heart. And when he went missing, the cops badgered me for any clue, as if I was supposed to do their damn job for them. All the while, you avoided me. You didn't call me for weeks after Christian left. Why? Why leave me too, Carey?"

I sigh as shame washes over me. "I felt terrible. I never thought he was serious about what he said, and then he did, and I didn't know what to say. Maybe I should have never told you anything."

"Sure! Let me think he just didn't love me enough to marry me. What kind of person thinks that way? You go around acting like you're all nice and sweet, but I know the truth. Oh, yeah. I know. I saw it firsthand after he left. You were nowhere to be found."

Even though I know another apology from me isn't going to help her, I say it anyway. "I'm sorry. I swear I never meant any harm. Please believe me, Jenna."

Nothing I'm saying is getting through to her, though.

"It all came together for me that night you and Emory came to Remington's. There you were, the heartbroken Carey we've all had to deal with since you found out that ex of yours cheated on you. I watched you from the kitchen and saw some guy who looked like he wanted to come over to the table. You're sitting there like some miserable, pathetic thing all broken up over some stupid guy, and another one was right there waiting in the wings. Meanwhile, what have I got these past few months? Nothing. You avoid me and leave me to my misery, and you get another chance at happiness? I don't think so. That's when I decided you needed to know what pain really felt like."

I listen to her explain the moment she decided to try to ruin my life, and all I can think of is how I never knew I'd hurt her so much. Before I can say anything, though, she quickly switches her focus.

"How has it felt having that cop constantly asking questions, making you feel like the villain, Carey? Now you know how I felt when they were at my door day in and day out asking where Christian went. Nothing like rubbing salt in the wound. First, he steals everything I have and abandons me, and then I get to talk about it over and over and over to a bunch of guys who acted like my feelings didn't matter. Well, they did! They mattered, and they should have mattered to you too, my good friend!"

She practically hisses those last words. My good friend.

"If you have a problem with me, why did you kill my

boss and my ex? Why make them pay for my being a terrible friend?" I ask, although I doubt in her state she could give me an answer that would clear any of this up for me.

"Two useless men," she says, waving the mention of them away like she's swatting a fly.

"Mr. James didn't deserve to die, Jenna. Neither did Chase."

A laugh explodes out of her that sounds purely manic. It frightens me and makes me think she's never going to let me get out of here alive now that I know everything.

"Trust me. That dick deserved to be killed months ago. That I waited shows a level of patience I honestly didn't know I had. You have no idea how many times he cheated on you and with dozens of other women. Christ, Carey. He even tried to sleep with me. Asshole thought we'd go find a quiet place and I'd let him get his rocks off. The joke was on him, though, because once we got to his favorite spot to take women, I climbed into the back seat and strangled him. The moron never saw it coming."

My chest aches at hearing her say Chase cheated on me that many times. "No matter what he did, he didn't deserve to die."

Jenna smiles and takes a step toward me before she stops. "What did you think of the doll's head I left when I was done? I figured there's no way those stupid cops would ever figure out this had to do with you if I didn't find some way to show them the same person killed that shithead boss of yours and your asshole ex-boyfriend."

"So the entire point was to make me look like the killer to the cops? Now what?"

My question seems to bother her, and sadness fills her expression. "What has to happen. They're gone, and now you will be too. Emory won't show. She's too busy with that muse of hers."

"You wrote those messages and letters that made it sound like I deserved the blame. You said so many terrible things."

She ignores me and shakes her head. "I wanted you to feel what I felt when Christian left me and then the cops looked at me like I was the bad guy. He steals all my money, and I'm the fucking villain. How can that be?"

"I never wanted you to feel like this, Jenna. I swear."

God, where the hell are Nicholas and the cops? I don't think I can keep her talking for much longer, and as soon as she stops, she's going to kill me.

"Well, not to worry, my best friend. I felt fantastic when I killed Christian. You wouldn't believe how good I felt. The utter and complete relief of knowing that a man who made your life miserable could never do it again."

Her confession that she killed her fiancé who stole all her money stuns me. "Is that why he left town and never came back?"

"Of course. You don't actually think he would have left his entire life without my getting rid of him. The guy knew I couldn't prove that money was mine since we had it in a joint bank account to pay for the wedding. No attorney would even consider taking the case as soon as they found out that little detail. So I didn't have a choice. I couldn't let him get away with stealing all that money and leaving me like I was some unwanted thing he could toss out like garbage. So I followed him one night and when he wasn't looking, I came up behind him and strangled the life out of the bastard. And to think he used to tease me because of my hands saying they were like a man's hands from all the work I do as a chef. That son of a bitch is lucky I didn't carve him up like a goddamned turkey. He would have deserved that too."

"But where is he? Everyone thinks he just ran away with your money."

Jenna shrugs like she isn't concerned with her ex-fiancé or where he's decomposing. "Out of sight. Out of mind. Like all men should be."

The horror of her words and how casually they come out makes me step back, but I immediately run into the wall. There's nowhere for me to go.

"When you told me about Nicholas not bothering to even call after you two slept together, I heard that same sadness in your voice that you got when you found out Chase cheated on you. I know what it sounds like because I hear it in my voice sometimes even now. I haven't been with anyone in months, but still I replay that day when I found out what Christian did and I hear that same goddamned sadness in my head! I didn't deserve that. I loved him, Carey. I didn't deserve what he did to me."

Tears fill my eyes at how she sounds right now. Jenna loved Christian like she never loved anyone before. He was everything to her. When they announced their engagement, she stood next to him beaming a smile from ear to ear. I'd never seen her happier.

And then when he stole all that money they saved up and left her, I didn't think she'd be able to go on. She lost so much weight because she refused to eat. She almost lost her job because she couldn't be in public without practically breaking down. What he did crushed her, and now I see it affected her far more than I ever knew.

"I'm sorry, Jenna. What happened to you was wrong. It was a betrayal of the love you gave Christian, and you didn't deserve that. But nobody deserved to die. We just have to go on, even when it's so hard you don't want to get out of bed in the morning. You need help. I'll be there for you when you get it too. I promise."

She laughs again, and this time I'm sure she's going to lose control any minute. "Help? For what? I'm finally in control of things. Of my life. Nobody screws me over anymore. Trust me, Carey. I'm finally happy again."

Although I know I might be in danger, I hope my dear friend won't hurt me, so I step out from behind the chair and open my arms. "It's okay, Jenna. I'm here for you. I promise. Emory will be too. We're the three musketeers, right?"

Jenna smiles and shakes her head. "You weren't there for me last time, so there won't be another chance for you."

I shudder in fear, but I have to try to defuse this situation. I don't want anyone else hurt. Not Jenna. Not me. The pain stops here.

"Please, Jenna. It doesn't have to be this way. You aren't this person. You're kind. You're better than me. I know that now."

Just then, my front door flies open and Jenna spins

around to look at Officer Thompson and Nicholas there, the cop with his gun drawn and pointed at her as she steps away from me.

"It's okay," I say, trying to make sure he doesn't use that weapon on her. "Jenna just needs some help. Please don't hurt her."

I turn to look at her and say, "It's okay, right? Nobody has to get hurt here."

She shakes her head and takes a step toward the patio doors and then another. "Again men make it worse. I know you meant what you said, but they don't. They're just going to ruin everything."

"No, I won't let them. I promise. Just let Officer Thompson do what he has to, and you can get help. It'll be okay. It will. When the police hear what happened to you, everyone will understand."

I look at her through tear-filled eyes as she opens the sliding glass door and backs out onto the balcony. I can't let her do this. She's one of my best friends, and even though she's done terrible things and needs help, she doesn't deserve to die.

Nobody did.

"Jenna, please. Come back in. Please!"

Nicholas runs over to me and holds me as Officer Thompson slowly walks across the room toward the patio doors. I watch as she backs away toward the balcony railing, as terrified now as I was a few seconds ago.

"Please put the gun away. Please!" I sob. "You're scaring her, and if you'd just put the gun away, she wouldn't be out there. She's not going to hurt anyone now."

My pleas fall on deaf ears, and the officer continues to practically stalk Jenna, his gun trained on her. "Jenna Snyder, you're under arrest for the attempted murder and assault of Nicholas Madera, the murder of Randall James, and the murder of Chase Kerrick. I need you to come back inside right now," Officer Thompson says in a calm voice.

But it doesn't work.

Jenna climbs up onto the railing and teeters for a moment as she gets her balance. I watch in horror as she looks at me and a tear slides down her cheek.

"No! Don't do it! Come back in, Jenna. Please. Don't do this!" I sob as Nicholas keeps me there in front of him.

A second later, she jumps, and before I know it, she's gone. I turn in utter sadness and begin to cry as Nicholas holds me.

"Why did she have to jump?" I ask as tears stream down my face. "All she had to do was come back in. I would have helped her. I would have been there for her this time."

"I know," Nicholas whispers against the top of my head.

Officer Thompson asks if I'm okay, and Nicholas tells him I'll be fine, but the truth is, I don't know if I'll ever be fine. One of my best friends killed two people because of me, and now she's dead.

I don't know how I can be fine after that.

26

A KNOCK on my front door makes my heart skip a beat, but I shake my head and push the memory of what happened away, at least for a few minutes. It's been three weeks since Jenna died, yet to this moment, dread fills me when I hear someone at my door.

I open it to see Officer Thompson standing in my hallway. Surprised he's come to my apartment since I haven't seen him since that terrible day, I stare at him for a long moment before I say, "Oh, hello. What are you doing here?"

Not exactly my nicest way of saying hi. I don't know why, but something about Officer Thompson makes me act not like myself.

"There's no need to worry, Miss Mitchell. I'm not here with any bad news. I just wanted to check on how you're doing," he says with a smile.

Stepping back, I nod and thank him. "Please, come in." Now that he's not constantly making me feel like I'm a suspect, I don't mind inviting him into my home.

He walks into my apartment and stops, turning around to face me. "So, how have you been?" he asks, and I get the sense he genuinely wants to know.

I close the door and shrug. "Okay, I guess. I think a big part of me still can't believe all that happened. I had no idea Jenna could do such terrible things."

Officer Thompson nods. "I understand. We found her fiancé's body. The coroner believes he died the same way Mr. James and Mr. Kerrick died. Strangulation."

All I can do is shake my head in disbelief. One of my best friends was a murderer three times over, and I never knew. Even worse, I never picked up on how much pain she must have been in for all that time. I have to believe that's why she did what she did. Jenna was never a cruel person. The world made her that way.

"I hated Christian for what he did to her, but even he didn't deserve what happened."

What else is there to say? That one terrible act of stealing from her set this entire horrible chain of events into motion. Christian was a bad person, a thoughtless man who had a lot coming to him, but not murder.

I can't help but admit that at least to Jenna, I shared the blame for all that happened too. God, how I wish I could go back and do so many things differently.

The officer falls silent, but a second knock on my door interrupts us and I hurry to answer it. Emory stands in my hallway wearing a big smile and holding a pizza box.

"I come bearing gifts. Well, one big gift with pepperoni and mushrooms. You better be hungry. I got the biggest pizza that place by my apartment offers."

She marches past me but stops dead when she sees

I'm not alone. "Officer Thompson, I didn't know you were here. Has Carey broken the law?" she asks with a flirty chuckle.

He smiles, and I instantly recognize there's something happening between the two of them. "Not that I know of," he answers.

"Well, I can't promise she's going to be good today. We've got a pizza and some margaritas, so there's no telling what we'll be up to later."

Quickly, I say, "We'll be good. Emory is just teasing. Honestly."

The last thing I need is Officer Thompson thinking he needs to keep an eye on me. He may be a nice guy now that he's not investigating anything that has to do with my life, but that doesn't mean I want him around.

My friend sets the giant pizza box on my counter and winks at the cop. "Maybe I'm teasing, and maybe I'm not. You'll have to come around later and check up on us to see."

Officer Thompson's grin grows bigger as she flirts with him. He really is an attractive man when he's not making my life miserable. There's something about the way his face lights up when he smiles.

"Well, I might have to do that," he says as he begins walking toward the door. "Have a nice day, ladies."

Before I can politely thank him for coming over to check on me, Emory blurts out, "Oh, we will, Officer Thompson."

Just as he's walking out to the hallway, he looks at her and says, "Wyatt."

Emory's eyes grow wide before she smiles and says,

"Well, Wyatt, maybe we'll have to cause a little trouble to get you back here. Nothing too bad. I promise."

He reaches into his pocket and pulls out his card to hand her. "Just in case you need anything. Have a good day, you two."

Before the door closes behind him, Emory's giggling like a schoolgirl with a new crush. "Wyatt. I like that name. It suits him, don't you think?"

I head over to the counter and open the pizza box to grab a slice for each of us. "I'm just happy he doesn't suspect me of anything. Now that he's not harassing me day and night about people dying around me, he's not a bad guy."

Emory takes a piece of pizza from me and rolls her eyes. "Not a bad guy? He's hot, especially in that uniform of his, and you know I have a thing for men like him."

As I take my first bite of our lunch, I laugh. "You mean men who are breathing?"

Suddenly, I realize after all that's happened that my comment is in bad taste. "That didn't come out like I meant it," I say quietly.

My friend waves off my unease. "Don't worry about it. It's not like you were the one killing people, Carey. What happened was because of Jenna, not you. There's no point in being all solemn for the rest of our lives."

"It's only been three weeks, Emory. You don't think it's too soon?"

She sits down on my sofa and shakes her head. "Too soon for what? Living like normal people? Flirting with hot guys? No. It's the perfect time for both, if you ask me."

Leave it to Emory to think three weeks is enough time to put all that's happened behind us.

"So, are you planning to see if something can happen with Officer Thompson?" I ask, unable to use his given name for some reason.

Smiling, she says, "Wyatt. You should call him by his first name since he could be Mr. Right for me."

I nearly drop my slice of pizza as I look at her in shock. "Mr. Right? You never talk about men that way. They're always Mr. Right Now, assuming you even bother telling us their names."

My use of that pronoun—us—comes out without me even thinking, but as soon as Emory and I hear it, the mood between us changes. We haven't really talked about what happened with Jenna. I have the feeling Emory either can't handle it yet or simply doesn't want to dwell on how horrible everything got.

As for me, it's all I could think about for the first week or so. Nicholas probably got tired of hearing me talk about it, but I needed to tell someone how it made me feel.

A rare, serious look settles into Emory's expression, and she lets out a heavy sigh. "You want to know something? I thought it was either her or Nicholas killing everyone."

I'm stunned for the second time in as many minutes. "Really? Nicholas or Jenna? Not me?"

"You couldn't hurt a fly, Carey. Even Wyatt knew that, I bet. He just needed to keep talking to you to help him figure out who it could be. When Nicholas was attacked, I knew it wasn't him, but I still couldn't wrap my head around the idea that Jenna could be the killer. I mean, yeah, she hated men, but I never dreamed that could mean she'd go around strangling them."

I sit down beside her on the sofa and sigh. "I miss her, you know? Yeah, I know what she did and how she blamed me, but she was our friend. I can't stand the idea that I missed how much pain she was in all that time. I feel so selfish. I wasn't there when she needed me."

Emory pats my leg and smiles. "Don't think that way. She never let on she was that unhappy. What happened isn't any fault of ours. Jenna had problems, obviously."

She stops and then adds, "But I miss her too."

After sitting silently for a while, Emory nudges me with her elbow. "Enough feeling down. Tell me about how things are going with that sexy boyfriend of yours. And don't leave out any details. I want to hear everything!"

I smile and tell her a few things Nicholas and I have been up to lately. Maybe Emory has the right idea with her attitude of living for the moment. It's never been my style, but I like to think I could be like that too.

What I know is I don't want to become mired down by anger or sadness like Jenna did. I owe it to the memory of those she took from us and to her to not become that person.

Look for K.M.'s next thriller, The Neighbor!

ABOUT THE AUTHOR

K.M. Scott loves a good story. A New York Times and USA Today bestselling author, K.M. has written dozens of books. In addition to romance, she's written cozy mysteries under her Anina Collins pen name. She lives in Pennsylvania with a herd of animals and when she's not writing can be found reading or feeding her TV addiction.

Be sure to visit K.M.'s Facebook page at **https://www.facebook.com/kmscottauthor** for all the latest on her books, along with giveaways and other goodies! And to hear all the news on K.M. Scott books first, sign up for her newsletter today and be sure to visit her website at **http://www.kmscottbooks.com**

ALSO BY K.M. SCOTT

HEART OF STONE SERIES
Crash Into Me (Heart of Stone #1)

Fall Into Me (Heart of Stone #2)

Give In To Me (Heart of Stone #3)

Heart of Stone Volume One

Ever After (Heart of Stone #4)

A Heart of Stone Christmas (Heart of Stone #5)

Return To Me (Heart of Stone #6)

Forever With Me (Heart of Stone #7)

Heart of Stone Volume Two

Hard As Stone (Heart of Stone #8)

Set In Stone (Heart of Stone #9)

Silent As A Stone (Heart of Stone #10)

Heart of Stone Volume Three

All of Me (Heart of Stone #11)

CLUB X SERIES
Temptation (Club X #1)

Surrender (Club X #2)

Possession (Club X #3)

Satisfaction (Club X #4)

Acceptance (Club X #5)

Complete Club X Series Box Set

NeXt SERIES

Notorious (NeXt #1)

Infamous (NeXt #2)

Ravenous (NeXt #3)

Ambitious (NeXt #4)

Flirtatious (NeXt #5)

Mysterious (NeXt #6)

Sensuous (NeXt #7)

Desirous (NeXt #8)

KING BROTHERS SERIES

Cruel King

Wild King

CORRUPTED LOVE TRILOGY

If I Dream (Corrupted Love #1)

If You Fight (Corrupted Love #2)

If We Fall (Corrupted Love #3)

Corrupted Love Trilogy Box Set

ADDICTED TO YOU SERIES

Crave (Addicted To You #1)

Adore (Addicted To You #2)

Shatter (Addicted To You #3)

Claim (Addicted To You #4)

Addicted To You Series Box Set

PROJECT ARTEMIS SERIES

In The Darkness (Project Artemis #1)

After The Storm (Project Artemis #2)

Behind The Scenes (Project Artemis #3)

Project Artemis Box Set

FINDING THE ONE SERIES

Hard Work (Finding The One #1)

Big Love (Finding The One #2)

DIRTY BOSS SERIES

Sweet Things (Dirty Boss #1)

Private Secretary (Dirty Boss #2)

Play Date (Dirty Boss #3)

Dirty Boss Volume One

BOOKS BY K.M. SCOTT WRITING AS GABRIELLE BISSET

SONS OF NAVARUS SERIES

Vampire Dreams Revamped (A Sons of Navarus Prequel)

Blood Avenged (Sons of Navarus #1)

Blood Betrayed (Sons of Navarus #2)

Longing (A Sons of Navarus Short Story)

Blood Spirit (Sons of Navarus #3)

The Deepest Cut (A Sons of Navarus Short Story)

Blood Prophecy (Sons of Navarus #4)

Blood Craving (Sons of Navarus #5)

Blood Eclipse (Sons of Navarus #6)

Blood Ascendant (Sons of Navarus #7)

The Sons of Navarus Box Set #1

The Sons of Navarus Box Set #2

DESTINED ONES DUET

Stolen Destiny (Destined Ones Duet #1)

Destiny Redeemed (Destined Ones Duet #2)

VICTORIAN EROTIC ROMANCES

Love's Master

Masquerade

The Victorian Erotic Romance Trilogy

COZY MYSTERIES UNDER ANINA COLLINS

POPPY MCGUIRE COZY MYSTERY SERIES

The Eleventh Hour

After Hours

Top of the Hour

The Darkest Hour

Happy Hour

The Witching Hour

The Finest Hour

Poppy McGuire Mysteries Box Set #1

Poppy McGuire Mysteries Box Set #2

www.ingramcontent.com/pod-product-compliance
Lightning Source LLC
LaVergne TN
LVHW090726050125
800550LV00039B/1054